The Caretaker of Lorne Field

The Caretaker of Lorne Field

Dave Zeltserman

The Overlook Press
New York

This edition first published in hardcover in the United States in 2010 by
The Overlook Press, Peter Mayer Publishers, Inc.
141 Wooster Street
New York, NY 10012
www.overlookpress.com

Cataloging-in-Publication Data is available from the Library of Congress

Book Design and type formatting by Bernard Schleifer
Manufactured in the United States of America
FIRST EDITION
ISBN 978-1-59020-303-3
10 9 8 7 6 5 4 3 2 1

To Jeff Michaels,
friends since second grade
and the best man at my wedding.

The Caretaker of Lorne Field

Chapter 1

Jack Durkin let out a groan as his wife, Lydia, dropped a bowl of corn flakes in front of him.

"Aw, woman," he moaned. "You trying to kill me? Corn flakes? This makes twenty-three days straight now."

"You don't like it? Get a job that pays money."

"*Get a job that pays money*," he said, mimicking her. "I got a job, you old hag—"

"Don't you dare call me that!"

"Well," he said, sniffing, "don't you make fun of my job then. I spend every day saving this world, and don't you forget it!"

She laughed at that. "Saving the world? You old fool, you spend all your time pulling out weeds from a field nobody cares about."

"Pulling out weeds?" he exclaimed with indignation. "Hell you say! I spend every goddamn day from winter thaw to first frost saving this worthless planet. Those ain't no weeds I'm pulling. They're Aukowies, as you damn well know! Weeds, huh? Do weeds scream every time you kill one of them?"

Lydia Durkin stopped scrubbing the previous night's dishes to roll her eyes. Half under her breath she muttered that he was nothing but an old fool.

"Old fool, am I? We'll see. Maybe I forget to pull one of them evil little suckers out, let it grow nice and big and hungry." Being as quiet as he could, he pushed himself away from the table and tiptoed over to her on his bare feet. Then, once within striking distance, he jabbed his fingers hard into her ribs, tickling her. "Nothing but one of them Aukowies eating you up," he laughed.

"Stop it! Stop it!" she screamed, jerking away and striking out with an elbow, catching him flush in his stomach. He stopped, and he stopped laughing, too.

"It's not funny," she said. "It's not funny us living like this. Because you have to spend every day walking up and down a field pulling weeds—"

"They're not weeds, you crazy old bat—"

"Shut up! I told you not to call me that! And I'm not old, only forty-six. I only look old 'cause I've been living with you like a pauper. Because you're too lazy to get a real job."

Jack Durkin held his stomach gingerly, still recovering having had his wind knocked out of him by that elbow. Damn thing was as hard as a crowbar. His knees felt creaky as he hobbled back to his chair. Without much enthusiasm he took a bite of corn flakes, then dropped his spoon back into the bowl.

"I got a job," he said defiantly. "The most frickin' important job in this whole goddamn world. And I'm under contract, goddamit!"

"You and your lousy contract."

"Don't you dare," he said, pointing a thick finger at her. "That contract is the most sacred piece of paper on the planet. Don't you dare desecrate it!"

Something about his tone stopped her. She went back to scrubbing the dishes and muttering under her breath what a useless fool she married. Jack Durkin sat scowling, first at her then at the bowl of corn flakes sitting in front of him. He pushed the bowl away, his round face turning red.

"Where are Lester and Bert? Why ain't my sons eating breakfast with me?"

"It's summer. I'm letting them sleep past six o'clock!"

"Well, that's not going to happen again. Tomorrow morning they're damn well joining me for breakfast. If I'm off saving the world every day, least they can do is join their pa for breakfast. You get them woken up or I'll drag them out of bed myself. Don't you think I won't! And quit your goddamn muttering!"

Fed up, he pushed himself away from the table, grabbed his baseball cap and thermos, and headed towards the door.

Lydia Durkin stared stone-faced at him, but once he opened the door she softened a bit. "Ain't you gonna eat nothin'?"

"Not in the mood now."

"Well, I'll bring you a lunch."

"No, you don't. It's in the contract, goddamit! You don't come out to Lorne Field. Never!"

He bent over and slipped his wool socks on and saw one of his toes sticking through the fabric. He glared at the toe angrily as if it had no right to be there, then put on his work boots. It took time tying up his laces, especially with how bad his back felt. When he was done he slowly straightened up, trying hard not to let Lydia see how much pain he was in, and with a loud harrumph stepped outside and slammed the door behind him.

Damn, that woman put him in a foul mood. Should be a law against her serving him corn flakes twenty-three straight days, especially her knowing that was all he'd have to eat until eight that night. And that little witch could've ruptured his spleen elbowing him the way she did. Chrissakes, all he was doing was being playful. As infuriating as all that was, what stuck in his craw was the way she belittled his job. Made it sound like he was some kind of loon.

Thinking about all that only made his foul mood blacker.

There was a time when the Caretaker of Lorne Field was held in reverence. When people respected the position and understood the sacrifices the Caretaker made so the rest of them could be safe. With his pa things started to change— slowly, maybe, but they changed as the ones who believed started to die off, and it had only grown worse under his tenure. Damn it, he had the most important job in the world, and now it was just one slight after the next. If not from his wife, then from the rest of the townsfolk. Even from his own boys . . .

Thinking of that made his back ache more than it had been.

Years of tending to Lorne Field left him with a rounded spine, bowed legs and creaky knees. All that bending and stooping he had to do all day long. Fifty-two years old and he felt like an old man. More than that, he looked like one. The sun had dried him out during all those years of walking back and forth across Lorne Field. Left his skin like a piece of rawhide. Probably responsible too for a good part of his hair falling out.

He stopped to work out the kink in his back. Bad enough he had creaky knees, now he had a kinky back. And if that weren't enough, he was reduced to walking on foot down the dirt path to Lorne Field because some delinquent punks stole his bike. He had asked Lydia to buy him a new one, but she refused, claiming they didn't have the money. When Chester Conley owned the town's sporting goods store he would've gladly given Durkin a free bike, but Chester had long since retired to Arizona, and his son who took over the shop didn't see things the way Chester had. Now Durkin was going to have to wait until the first frost to figure out how he would raise enough money for a new bike, which left him stuck having to walk for the rest of the season. One more indignity piled upon all the rest. One more stinking burden to shoulder.

A black, black thought entered his head. He could teach them all a lesson. If he bought a bus ticket, he could be in California in three days. Probably take eight, maybe nine days for the Aukowies to mature, another week or so for them to ravage the land and make their way to the west coast. That'd give him more than two weeks of peace and quiet. Two weeks without some raisin-faced shrew picking the flesh off his tired old carcass. Two weeks without his ungrateful boys rolling their eyes and smirking at him. Best of all, two weeks without any condescending looks from those townsfolk when he walked past them. Oh boy, would that teach them! Let them see how funny their jokes were when Aukowies shred them into mincemeat! Of course the Aukowies would get his wife and boys first, not only because they were closest but 'cause of the grudge they held against him. They'd make 'em suffer. Probably take their time too, at least as much as an Aukowie could.

He imagined Lydia and his boys in the grasp of the Aukowies, imagined the pure horror that would blind their eyes as they realized how all his stories weren't just stories. As he visualized it, his thoughts turned into a lead weight that sunk into his gut. As much as he would never admit it, he did care for his battle-axe of a wife and his two gangly teenage boys.

That's right, you old fool, he thought to himself. Teach the world a lesson by destroying it.

Whether or not the rest of the town still understood it, his position was one of the greatest responsibility. He had never yet forsaken it, and he wasn't about to. No matter how miserable the weather was, no matter how poorly he felt, he had been out there every day since his twenty-first birthday doing his job as stipulated by the contract. Even when he was nearly dead with pneumonia he was out tending Lorne Field. Lydia had been near hysterical trying to get him to the hospital, but he wouldn't be deterred. Stayed there seven in the morning to seven at night as he always did. Even though he was almost blind from fever and had chipped a tooth 'cause he was shaking so bad, he weeded out the Aukowies and kept the world safe. Took him two years to lose the cough that pneumonia had given him. But he did his job.

Straightening his back as best he could, he pushed out his chin and quickened his pace as he headed to Lorne Field. If he didn't let that sickness stop him, he sure as hell wasn't going to let feeling sorry for himself do it now.

Lydia sat deep in thought, a cigarette held loosely between her index and middle fingers, her small bloodshot eyes watering from the smoke. She couldn't help feeling guilty sending her fool husband out of the house once again with nothing but cold cereal. You'd think he'd catch on that it was no accident it'd been weeks since he had anything decent to eat. That maybe, just maybe, he'd realize she was trying to discourage him from this joke of a life they were living and push him into a real job making real money. But the man was as dense as a brick. He actually sounded as if he believed the nonsense he spouted off about saving the world each day. Well, if he was going to deprive them of a real life then she was going to deprive him of real food!

Absentmindedly, she noticed her cigarette had burnt close to her fingers. She stubbed it out, stared for a moment at the darkened yellow nicotine stain that ran along the inside of her index and middle fingers, and then lit up a fresh one. She wouldn't be smoking three packs a day if she didn't have to suffer such a fool of a husband! Nineteen years old when she got involved with him. How could she have known any better? Only nineteen years old . . . just barely out of high school . . .

Back then the Durkins were mostly a mystery to her. This odd little family that mostly kept to themselves. She remembered as a little girl the way her pa would seize up when he'd run into old man Durkin, almost as if he were in the presence of royalty. If they were in the diner, her pa would offer to buy him a beer or a sandwich. If they were in the street or the Country Store, her pa would ask if he could do anything for him. It never occurred to her as a child that her pa and old man Durkin were the same age. Old man Durkin seemed ancient in comparison, with his white hair and weather-beaten face and hunched-over appearance.

After high school she went to work as a waitress at the Main Street Diner. It was well into the following winter that Jack Durkin started to come in. He was the Caretaker of Lorne Field then and living alone at the Caretaker's cabin, his old man having retired to Florida and his younger brother, Joe, disappearing to God knows where. Growing up, she never had much to do with either of the Durkin boys. Joe was closer to her in age, but he mostly kept to himself in school. Jack was six years older but, like his brother, didn't talk much to other folk, and the few times she'd see him around town he walked about as if he carried a heavy weight strapped to his back.

During those winter months Jack became a regular at the diner and Lydia soon caught him sneaking peeks at her. Not that she minded. At this point only a little bit of the fatigue of being Caretaker showed on his face. He was fairly decent looking, still had his hair, his back mostly straight and his chest only showing slight signs that someday it would cave in from all the stooping he had to do. Anyway, he didn't let his hands roam along her backside like a lot of the men in the diner, and after three weeks of her trying to look shy and him pretending that he wasn't openly staring at her, he asked her out and she accepted.

He took her to a nice restaurant two towns over in Hamilton. They both had lamb chops and he ordered a bottle of red wine and the waiter didn't bother to check her driver's license to see that she was two years under the legal drinking age. He didn't talk much during dinner, mostly looked down at his hands or through the window at the snow falling outside. Around the time when they were eating parfait desserts and drinking coffee with Amaretto, he cleared his throat and asked whether she knew he was Caretaker of Lorne Field.

"Well, yes. I suppose everyone back home knows that."

"Any idea what I do as Caretaker?"

She thought about it, shrugged. "I guess you take care of Lorne Field."

He smiled at that. It was a mean-spirited smile confined mostly to his mouth; his eyes reflected something other than humor. She didn't like it at all. "That's one way of putting it," he said. "You know much else about it?"

She shook her head.

"You know anything about the contract?"

Again she shook her head.

"My family's been under contract for almost three hundred years now. That's nine generations of Durkins. Contract calls for the Caretaker to live freely in the home at Lorne Meadow and to be paid eight thousand dollars as an honorarium each year."

"*Honorarium*—that's like a salary?"

"Yep."

"You get paid eight thousand dollars a year and get to live rent-free just for taking care of a field?"

His face darkened for a moment, but it passed. "That's right," he said, his voice strained. "Look, I don't have time to do this right. In a few months I got to be back working every day seven in the morning to seven at night and I'll be doing that until first frost, so I don't have time to court a woman right. The contract requires me to get married and have a son, preferably two in case something happens to the older boy. I don't have time to be messing around. You're no beauty but you're pleasant enough to look at. So you want to marry me?"

At first all she could do was stare at him open-jawed, then she found her voice and sputtered, "On our first date you're going to propose to me? And that's how you're going to do it? By telling me I'm no beauty?"

She could almost see him swallow back the crack, '*Well, you ain't!*' His face reddened slowly as he looked back at her. "Look, I don't got time to do this right. I apologize if I offended you. I ain't socialized much in my life. I guess in your own way you're pretty. But I told you I don't got time to do this the way it should be done. Contract requires me to get married and have a son and it's got to be done soon. You don't want to, that's fine, just tell me. I got my eye on other girls, you just the nicest."

That last comment appeased her pride enough for her to answer back, "Well, you ain't so good-looking yourself."

"Never said I was, did I!"

"Well, least you could do is propose right!"

"I don't got time for that!" But he got up off his chair, moved next to her and slowly lowered one knee to the floor, grimacing as he did so. After taking a ring from his pocket, he cleared his throat and looked like he needed to spit something out. "Lydia May Jones, will you marry me?" he asked, sliding the ring on her finger.

She examined the ring and told him it looked old-fashioned.

"It should," he said. "It's an antique. Been in my family over two hundred years."

"How big do you suppose it is?" she asked, one eye closed as she squinted hard at the ring. "At least half a carat? I heard rings are supposed to be at least half a carat."

"I don't know. So what's your answer? You gonna marry me?"

"I'll think about it."

He shot her a look like he wanted to smack her, but he got off his knee, sat back down and silently finished his parfait and coffee.

When he took her home later, he walked her to the front door and then grumbled that he needed an answer soon. "Contract requires me to get married. I don't got time to wait. You don't want to then that's that. I'll just have to find someone else. Other girls I got my eye on."

"I'll tell you tomorrow."

He nodded, not happy with her answer but willing to accept it for the time being. As he started back to his car, she stopped him. "Least you could do is kiss me goodnight!"

Awkwardly, he moved back to her and gave her a quick peck on the cheek. She was surprised at how strong his fingers were as he held her by her shoulders. Like they could crush stone. Bricklayer's hands, that's what she thought. She took hold of him by the side of his face and had him give her a proper kiss.

"So what do you do as Caretaker?" she asked in a breathless whisper.

He smiled then. Not the mean-spirited smile she had seen earlier, but something sad, maybe a bit whimsical. "I save the world everyday. Break my back doing it, too."

When she got inside she showed her pa the engagement ring and told him about the proposal.

"It's a nice-looking ring," her pa said.

"It's old looking," she said, pouting. Then forcing her voice to quaver with indignation, she added, "The nerve of that man. Proposing to me on the very first date. And the way he did it!"

Her pa thought about it and showed a conciliatory smile. "Well, first off, that ring's an antique. Probably worth a lot of money. And I wouldn't be too hard on the boy about how he proposed. He probably don't have time to do things otherwise."

"What's that mean?"

He ignored the question, a weariness aging his large broad face. "You should think about marrying him, Lydia. He's got a hard road ahead of him and could use the help of a good wife."

"Why should I even consider it with the low class way he treated me? And what's so hard about his road? All he does is take care of a field!"

He sighed, kissed her on the forehead and started to walk away. She yelled out to him, "Pa, you didn't answer me. What's so hard about taking care of a field?" All he did in response was wave a tired hand in the air before disappearing into his bedroom.

Contrary to what she told her pa, she had pretty much already made up her mind to marry Jack Durkin. She was sick of waitressing; it was tough on her ankles and every night she came home with her feet all blistered and swollen. Besides, in 1979 eight thousand dollars a year was a good salary, better than what a lot of people made when you include having your home for free. It seemed like a good deal, one that she decided she couldn't pass up. The next morning when Jack Durkin came to ask for her answer she told him she'd marry him, and Durkin, still frowning, nodded and told her he'd arrange the wedding. Three weeks later they were married.

After they were husband and wife he showed her the Caretaker's contract. The document was several hundred years old, and he was so earnest as he went over it that she almost burst out laughing. But she decided if he could play his part with this foolishness so could she, especially if it meant free housing and eight thousand dollars a year. Even though the contract forbade anyone but the Caretaker or his eldest son from coming within a crow's flight (whatever that was?) of Lorne Field, she followed him one day and hid and watched as he walked up and down the field picking out weeds. When the canvas sack he carried was filled he dumped out its contents into a stone pit and continued with his weeding. After an hour of watching that, she got bored and headed back to their house with no interest in ever watching him at work again.

For the first ten years or so of their marriage she had no real complaints, although she didn't much care for her husband's hardened attitude towards her three miscarriages, acting as if it didn't matter because the babies would've been girls. And she didn't like the fact that months before she found out she was pregnant with Lester he had acted all nutty, mumbling stuff about how if she didn't have a boy soon he'd have to divorce her—that it was stated so in the contract. But other than that cold behavior on his part things were okay. More than just the house being free, people did things for them during those first ten years. Doc Wilson never charged for medical care, old man Langston who owned the local butcher shop gave them their meat for free, and others helped them out, too. Lewis Black came by and did free carpentry. Tom Harrold the same with plumbing. Ed Goodan for the electrical. There was little she had to pay for during those first ten years. And there were times when Jack, in his own gruff way, acted kind of sweet with her.

About the time she was pregnant with Lester things started to change. Doc Wilson died and the new doc who took over started to charge them full price. Several years later when old man Langston passed the butcher shop on to his son, he made him promise to continue giving the Durkins their meat free. The son did for a while but after the old man moved down south he went back on his word. Over time most of those who'd been helping out were either dead or retired elsewhere, and the ones who took their places didn't have the old generosity. Worse, she started noticing townsfolk looking at her funny, like they knew all about the scam she and Jack were running on them. Before too long the eight thousand dollar annual honorarium didn't seem like much, even with the free housing—especially after Bert was born and they had two hungry boys to feed. The last few years they were barely able to scrape by. Pipes, water heater, furnace—something always seemed to need fixing in that old house, and she couldn't afford to take the boys to the doctor anymore, let alone have their crooked teeth fixed. She had gotten to the point where she was just worn out from it. Hell, welfare would pay more than what they were getting.

The last cigarette she lit had mostly burnt out. She took several last puffs from it and crushed it out in the saucer she used as an astray. She heard some scuffling noises behind her and turned and saw her two boys. Both were thin as string beans with alfalfa-like hair that seemed to shoot in all directions. Lester was seventeen and already over six feet tall. With the way Jack stooped, the boy appeared to tower over his father. Bert was thirteen and short for his age—barely topping five feet. Both boys physically took after her, Bert maybe more so than Lester.

Bert scratched the back of his head as he yawned. Lester stared at her sullenly and sniffed. "Dad already left to pull weeds?"

Lydia nodded. "You two boys want breakfast?"

Lester rolled his eyes. "Well, yeah, that's what we're here for." Bert joined her at the small kitchen table and flashed a good-natured smile. It tore her up to see either of them smile with the way their teeth looked, almost as if cherry bombs had gone off in their mouths leaving them twisted and criss-crossing over each other. It killed her that she couldn't afford braces for her boys.

"How'd you two like blueberry pancakes and bacon?" she asked. Lester, making a snuffling noise, said it was okay with him. Bert just smiled hungrily and rubbed his stomach. She got up and found the bacon, blueberries and eggs that she had hidden in the refrigerator behind a bottle of prune juice and a head of wilted cabbage. All she had to do was put things where they didn't belong and her husband would never find them, lacking even that much imagination. She brought the items back to the counter, and along with some milk and flour, started mixing the pancake batter.

Lester said sourly, "You know what nickname they started calling me yesterday? Weedpuller. It really sucks being in this family."

"Les, honey, I'm sorry. Just ignore them."

"Weedpuller!" Bert yelled out. "Ha!"

Lydia shot him a look that silenced him, then went back to stirring the batter. After a long moment Lester asked if he was really going to have to become the Caretaker when he turned twenty-one.

"No, honey, you won't."

"'Cause I don't want to do that. Spend all day pulling weeds like some retard."

"You ain't going to have to."

"Dad keeps saying I will. That it's in his stupid contract."

Lydia turned, her eyes hot enough to have ignited a can of gasoline. "That contract can go to blazes," she said.

Chapter 2

Each morning Jack Durkin would make a quick walk through the woods bordering Lorne Field before starting his weeding. He never found any Aukowies growing there and didn't suppose he ever would. Those suckers probably had to grow up straight, either that or they didn't have sense to try to find a less obvious place to push up out of the ground —but you'd think after three hundred years they'd catch on that coming up into Lorne Field wasn't doing them any good. Or maybe they just wanted to do it on their own terms, expecting to eventually wear down the generations of Durkins who weeded them out. He knew looking through the woods was a waste of time, but it had become a matter of habit with him so he performed his morning ritual and, as usual, found the area free of Aukowies.

Standing at the edge of Lorne Field he gazed out and saw thousands of the little suckers already pushing themselves up out of the ground, maybe two inches high already. Even at that height they could take off a finger if you weren't careful. And if you were to trip and fall to the ground, they'd slice you to ribbons before you could get up. Aukowies grew fast, as much as a foot in one day. Come dusk they stop, almost as if they needed to rest for the night. Then the next dawn they'd start growing all over again.

There was no movement among the Aukowies. When they were that small they played possum and tried to act as if they were nothing but weeds. Most people looking at them would think they were nothing but an odd little weed. But Jack Durkin knew differently. If he squinted right, he could make out their evil little faces in their offshoots, and he knew those little pincers were more than thorns. He'd watch them wait until there was a wind, then pretend they were swaying in it, all the while really trying to wiggle themselves further out of the ground. They were clever little suckers, Jack Durkin had to give them that. Once they got to two feet in height, they wouldn't bother with their act. At that size they'd be whipping about as if they were caught in hurricane gales, not giving a damn about keeping up their masquerade. Jack Durkin never let one grow that high, but he'd heard stories from his pa about it. According to his pa it took hours to subdue several of them that had gotten to that height, having to first throw boulders on top of them to pin them down.

According to the Book of Aukowies, eight days would be all one needed to mature and break free from the ground. One mature Aukowie would wreak havoc, a field of them would ravage the world in a matter of weeks.

The thought often struck him about what would happen if he ever got laid up in the hospital or simply dropped dead of a heart attack. At fifty-two it could happen. His family was of tough stock—which was one of the reasons the Durkins were awarded the contract in the first place—but the responsibility of weeding Aukowies took its toll. It had aged him well beyond his years. Lester came around later in life than he should've. The caretaker position should've been passed on to a first-born son a decade earlier. As it was it would be another four years before Lester would turn twenty-one, and until that happened, Jack Durkin would just have to hope that he didn't suffer any major calamities or get hit by a bus or lightning or any number of other things that could lay him out. If he did, the end of the world would come soon after. He peered up at the sun for a moment, then went into the shed his great grandpa had built, took a canvas sack, a pair of leather gloves and a few gardening instruments from it and went to work.

Weeding the Aukowies was tricky. You had to make sure to keep your fingers away from their little pincers. Given a chance they'd spring to life and cut one off. You also had to be careful how you plucked them from the ground. Kind of feel your way to know which angle to pull at. When you did it right, and Jack Durkin almost always did it right, you'd pull out a thin root-like thing that ran a foot or so. He knew it wasn't any root, not with the sickly-sweet smell he'd be able to catch a faint whiff of, or the shrill little death scream that he could hear when the air was perfectly still. If you pulled the Aukowie out wrong you'd only break it off at the stem leaving the root-like thing feeding what was left. It would still make a shrill little noise—to Jack Durkin it would sound more like a rage-filled cry than anything else, and next time it came up the stem would be tougher, thicker, and you'd better be all the more careful pulling the damn thing from the ground 'cause you wouldn't get another chance after that. Durkin could sometimes go a whole season without pulling one wrong. When he did screw up, he'd mark where he made his mistake, then make sure next chance he had he'd pull the thing up right. As if his life depended on it.

After thirty-one years of weeding Lorne Field, he usually needed no more than a few seconds with an Aukowie, his hands deftly finding the right spot on the weed to grab, and almost instinctively knowing which angle to yank it so it slid out easily from the ground. Still, with thousands of these Aukowies pushing up, it would take him close to four hours to complete a full pass of the field. By the time he was done a second wave of Aukowies would be waiting for him. Maybe not as many as when he first arrived, but with the added fatigue factored in, his next pass would take close to another four hours. Add the same for his third and final pass. By then the Aukowies would be done for the night.

He had walked back and forth length-wise three times across the field pulling out hundreds of Aukowies, hearing them all screaming shrilly as they died, when he came across what at first sight looked like a daisy. He stood disoriented for a moment, blinking and wiping the sweat from his eyes. He had never before seen a flower growing in that field of death, and the fact that one could actually survive out there buoyed his spirits. Actually made him feel good. He stared at it, admiring it, until he realized what he thought were petals were actually groups of pincers turned inside out.

Up to new tricks, you little bugger, he thought.

With the toe of his work boot he nudged the thing. It didn't take the bait, though, staying perfectly still and maintaining its daisy-like camouflage.

Durkin crushed the Aukowie under the heel of his boot. He imagined the thing struggling now, but it had no chance. He reached down and got a good hold of the Aukowie by its stem. Feeling for the right angle to pull at, he lifted his foot and in the same motion yanked the damn thing as hard as he could. The root-like thing ripped out of the ground. He had the sense for a second of sniffing anti-freeze. More like he could taste it in the back of his throat. Durkin shoved the remains of the daisy-like Aukowie into his canvas sack.

"Ain't nothin' here but a bunch of weeds, huh?" he said bitterly.

A light breeze came up, and the Aukowies seemed to answer him by swaying to it. He could swear they were moving faster than they should've given the breeze that was blowing. Durkin knew the sound of his voice grated on these Aukowies. He knew it drove them crazy, and it took every bit of restraint they had not to react to it.

"What other tricks you got up your sleeve?" he yelled out, which made the Aukowies sway just that much faster, at least to his eye.

"Yeah, well," he muttered, "whatever you got it ain't good enough. Just ain't good enough, you dirty little buggers."

He stood still for a moment to catch his breath. Then as the Aukowies' swaying slowed a beat and became more in sync with the breeze that was blowing, Jack Durkin continued his weeding.

🌿

Lydia stood at the kitchen sink scrubbing the breakfast dishes. Both boys had finished eating and were out doing God knows what, but that was fine with her. They should be out having some fun, at least somebody in that house should be. A sour taste flooded her mouth as she thought how her life had become nothing but drudgery. Cleaning, sewing clothes, scraping by and most of all, worrying. Worrying about how she was going to juggle the bills coming in, how her boys were being deprived of what they deserved and how little she was able to have for herself. A knock on the back door shook her out of her dark thoughts. She left the sink to find Helen Vernon standing outside on the back porch.

The Caretaker of Lorne Field 29

"Thought maybe you could use some company," Helen said through the screen door.

Lydia opened the door to let her friend in. "I'll put on some coffee," she said.

Helen Vernon was a few years older than Lydia but looked ten years younger. Chunky, with blond hair, rosy cheeks and a mouth that was too big for her face. She and Lydia had been friends since grammar school, and she was the only friend Lydia still had who came out to visit. Helen sat at the table while Lydia took a coffee maker out from one of the bottom cabinets. As far as Jack was concerned the coffee maker had broken months ago—at least that's what she told him. Since then the only coffee she'd been serving him was an instant brand that tasted like watered-down mud, but when he wasn't around she made a nice French roast for herself.

After she started the coffee brewing, she joined her friend at the table and offered a cigarette. Helen accepted and both women lit up. They sat silently for a minute as they inhaled deeply on their cigarettes and sent smoke spiraling up between them.

"I'm just so damn tired of this," Lydia said.

Helen blew a stream of smoke out from the corner of her wide mouth. "You talk more to Jack about finding a real job?"

"Yeah, I talked to him until I was blue in the face." She laughed bitterly, her thin lips curling with spite. "The damn fool has his contract. He's out there saving the world every-day, don'cha know?"

"That's what he says to you?"

"Exact words."

The coffee had finished brewing. Lydia got up and poured two cups. She drank hers black while Helen filled hers a third of the way with milk and added several tea-spoons of sugar. Her eyes looked thoughtful as she sipped her coffee between drags of her cigarette.

"Maybe he's been playing the part so long he believes it," Helen said.

"Maybe. I don't know. All I know is he ain't giving this up. I'm near starving him to death and it don't seem to matter. He's going to go every day to that damn field to pick out those weeds. It don't matter to him that his family's living the way we are. I just don't know what to do about it."

"I still don't know why you won't divorce him."

Lydia looked at her friend with exasperation. "How am I gonna do that? He don't make enough to pay alimony. Where am I gonna live with my boys? Move back in with my parents? And what am I gonna do? I'm forty-six, my looks are gone, used up, and I got two teenage boys to feed and clothe. Nobody else for me to go to. The only way out is for that damn fool husband of mine to give up this foolishness and get himself a real job. I just don't see that happening."

Helen took a lazy drag on her cigarette and let the smoke tumble out her nose. Coolly, she said, "What if the town revokes his contract?"

"What do you mean?"

"Contracts can be revoked, can't they?"

"I still don't get you."

"It's simple," Helen said. "I don't think too many people here like the idea of paying eight thousand dollars a year to have some dope pull weeds from a field out in the middle of nowhere." She showed an apologetic smile. "Of course it could also mean you losing this house."

"Be a real shame to lose this house," Lydia said, the muscles hardening along her jaw. "No cable TV, no air conditioning, plumbing don't work half the time. Dank and cold in the winter, hot as blazes in the summer. Yeah, it would be a real shame." She noticed her cigarette had burnt down to mostly ash and filter and stubbed it out. "How do you suppose I could get the town to do something like that?"

"I don't think it would be too hard. I'm sure most people wouldn't be too happy spending our tax money like this, if they were properly reminded. I could start making some noise about it. Maybe you could inflame things yourself by going around town bragging about how easy you got it. You know, free house and money for doing nothing. I could raise the issue of canceling that contract at the next town council meeting."

A weariness showed in Lydia's face as she considered her friend's suggestion. The hardness around her mouth softened and her skin color paled to a dead fish color.

"I don't know," she said. "I'll have to think about it."

Helen covered one of Lydia's bony hands with a large fleshy one of her own. "Lydia, honey, that's just normal nervousness on your part. But if Jack's given no other choice, he'll land on his feet and get a real job. I'm sure in no time he'll be making three or four times what he's making now and you'll be able to live a more normal life. So what do you say, honey, should I start the ball rolling?"

Lydia's small gray eyes seemed lost as she stared into a corner of the room. As if coming out of a trance, she looked back at her friend and shook her head. "Give me a few days to think about it," she said.

The four teenage boys had snuck into Lloyd Jasper's vegetable garden and were loading a shopping bag with ripe tomatoes when the retired schoolteacher stepped outside, a scowl developing slowly over his heavily-lined face.

"What the hell you boys doing back there!" he yelled out as he squinted in their direction.

The four teenagers started running, the bag only half-filled. Sam Parsons tried holding four tomatoes against his stomach as he sprinted away. Two of them fell loose. He ignored them and kept running.

"Don't think I don't recognize you!" Lloyd Jasper yelled out at them. "Tony Morelli, I see you. You too, Sam Parsons. And you other two, I know who you are! Don't think I won't be calling your parents!"

Before too long the boys were out of earshot of the retired schoolteacher. They kept running until they reached the woods bordering Crystal Pond where they had stashed their bikes. Panting hard from the run, they caught their breaths and consolidated the tomatoes Sam Parsons and Lester Durkin carried off with the half-filled shopping bag Tony Morelli had under his thick arm. Morelli leered at Lester and said, "So Weedpuller, you still in on this, right? You're not backin' down 'cause we've been made by that old prick, right?"

Lester's mouth turned sullen. "Fuck you. I'm doing this. And quit calling me Weedpuller."

"You do this, you lose that name. Until then you're Weedpuller. Right, Sam?"

"Exactly." Sam Parsons smiled nervously, his face flushed with perspiration. "Weedpuller does this with us, he gets a new name."

Morelli winked at Carl Ashworth. "You agree, too?"

"Fuck, yeah," Carl said.

"Then what the fuck are we waiting for?" Morelli asked

gleefully, a malicious gleam shining in his dark eyes. He pulled his bike off the ground and rode off, carrying the bag full of tomatoes. The other boys got on their bikes and followed. Morelli led the way along the dirt path around the pond, then across woods until they reached the road leading to the Caretaker's cabin. As they rode past the cabin Lester lowered himself on his bike and tried to shield his face from view, hoping neither Bert or his mom saw him. When Morelli pulled onto the path leading to Lorne Field, he turned back to leer at his companions, then raced on until he pulled up to the edge of Lorne Woods.

The other three boys caught up to him and they divvied up the tomatoes. Lester Durkin, Sam Parsons and Carl Ashworth all took off their shirts and used them as makeshift sacks to carry theirs while Morelli held onto the bag. Morelli pointed out where in the woods he wanted each of his co-conspirators to go. "You know how far it is to the field?" he asked Lester. Morelli's round dark face was frozen in a heavy leer, but a wavering in his eyes betrayed his bravado. Lester shrugged and told him he had no idea.

"You've never been there before?"

"No. What made you think I would have?"

"I don't know. I would've thought your old man would've taken you sometime." Morelli paused before showing a nasty smirk. "After all, he's got to teach you how to pull weeds since you are the Weedpuller. But I guess you get practice pulling your own weed every night when you're alone."

Lester tried shoving Morelli but didn't budge him. "Quit calling me that!"

"You try that again," Morelli said, "and I'll shove one of these tomatoes down your throat. Understand?"

Carl Ashworth put an arm around Morelli's thick frame and guided him to the side. "Come on, man," Carl said, "this is going to be fucking awesome. Let's just get to it."

Morelli glared menacingly at Lester before turning to Carl Ashworth and Sam Parsons. "Stay hidden until the signal, okay?" He hesitated for a moment, and then looked back at Lester, a tenseness momentarily weakening his smirk.

"You're sure the field's this way?" Morelli asked.

"That's the direction my dad heads off every morning," Lester said.

With that the four of them ran into the woods, moving quickly at first, then slowing down as they crept closer to the field. Lester tried to keep low to the ground and hidden behind trees and rocks. After a while he could see the field and his dad in the middle of it. He tried keeping even closer to the ground as he edged forward, crawling to a thick oak tree sitting on the edge of the field. When he got to the tree he hid behind it, his heart beating like a drum in his chest, pounding so hard it felt like it was going to explode out of him. But the wild panic he felt at first was replaced by humiliation as he watched his dad walking up and down that field pulling weeds. He wanted to run up to his dad and pummel him for making him such a joke to his friends but he stayed where he was, tears flooding his eyes as he watched his dad work his way up and down the field, moving a little closer with each pass.

When his dad was within ninety feet of him Morelli threw the first tomato. It whistled past his dad's ear. That was the signal, and it brought a hail of tomatoes flying at his dad. One hit him flush in the jaw, another took his baseball cap off, a half dozen more hit him in the body. As the tomatoes splattered off him he almost tumbled over, then he turned to face them, his eyes dumb as if he had no clue what was happening. Furious over the ridiculousness of his dad, Lester started throwing his tomatoes, missing wildly several times before hitting his dad square in the nose with one. It almost knocked his dad off his feet but he recovered his footing and shook his fist in Lester's direction.

"You dumb asses!" his dad yelled, his face a bright red, partly from the tomatoes, mostly from blinding rage. "You're violating the contract! Goddamn you all!"

By then Lester was crying. Crying from the humiliation, disgust and fear. He could hear his friends laughing like hyenas as they took off back to their bikes. With tears streaming down his face, Lester ran after them.

At first Jack Durkin was too mad to see straight. Those juvenile punk bastards. Sneaking up on him like that to pelt him with tomatoes. This was how they were going to show their gratitude for him saving their sorry asses each day? This was the respect they had for him? And goddamn it, they violated the contract! Didn't they know what they were messin' with? All he wanted to do was chase them down and beat the living tar out of each and every one of them. Even after he wiped away the tomato all he could see was a thick red haze. When this haze finally lifted and he could see straight again, he took several steps towards the woods but stopped cold when he realized what was left of the tomatoes thrown at him were lying among the Aukowies.

He turned and stared in horror, knowing the Aukowies were sucking the juices out of the tomato remains. In the dead still air, he was sure he could hear the slurping noises they made. For a long moment he stood paralyzed and watched.

Those damn fools, he thought. Didn't they know they'd be feeding these Aukowies? With good reason the contract don't allow food to be brought onto Lorne Field. Goddamn reckless fools!

He snapped out of whatever trance he had fallen into and quickly touched his face, then checked his fingers to make sure he wasn't bleeding. According to the *Book of Aukowies*, human blood drove Aukowies wild with desire and made them grow like crazy. With some relief he saw that the only wet sticky stuff dripping from his face was juice from the tomatoes. He grabbed away from the Aukowies whatever tomato pieces they hadn't absorbed yet and made a note of which ones had most likely feasted on the tomatoes. He focused his weeding efforts on them. They were already stronger and tougher than they should've been at that height. He had to be more careful with them, first pinning them under his foot, then digging around them so he could get a better grip of their root. He was amazed at how much thicker they had gotten and how much more muscle he had to use to pull them out of the ground, but eventually he got them all.

When he was done he picked up his baseball cap. A large rip had split it. Scowling at the cap, he shoved it into his back pocket, then scoured the field to make sure all the tomato pieces had been picked up and that no nourishment was left behind for the next wave of Aukowies.

Standing there, he felt exhausted. He touched his nose and winced. His hand shook as he moved it down to his jaw and felt how hard and swollen the area was where he'd been hit. *Damn those punk kids to hell*, he thought. The whole incident left him worn out and tired. His knees buckled a bit, his legs feeling as if bags of wet sand had been tied to them. All he wanted to do was to lie down somewhere and take a nap. He looked out at the remaining section of the field that still needed weeding, and then back at the rest of the field already showing new Aukowies sprouting out. Sighing heavily he lifted his sack over his shoulder and continued with his day's work.

Chapter 3

Jack Durkin's day usually ended at seven, but it wasn't until eight o'clock that night he finished his third pass of the field and emptied the sack into a stone pit behind Lorne Field, adding to the small mountain of Aukowies picked earlier that day. Kerosene wasn't needed. Just throw a match on the Aukowie remains and they lit up as if they'd been soaked in gasoline. The contract required him to watch them burn, so after setting a match to the remains, he stood and watched the flames shoot skyward. After the fire died out he gathered up the ashes, mixed them with lime and buried them. Then he headed home.

At a quarter to nine Durkin stepped through his front door, too bone-tired at first to do anything but glare angrily at his wife. He would've fallen over when he took off his work boots except he was able to throw out his right hand and grasp the wall and keep himself on his feet. Lydia's color paled to a dead white as she watched him.

"What happened to you?" she asked, her voice unusually brittle.

He shot her a withering look, then hobbled past her and collapsed into a worn imitation-leather recliner that had been patched up in places with duct tape.

"You ain't going to tell me what happened?" Lydia demanded, a hot white anger chasing out whatever concern she had felt moments earlier.

"Get me a bucket of hot water first," Durkin said. "My

damn feet are swollen to twice their size."

"Oh, no! You tell me what happened or you just sit there and rot! I've been worrying half to death the last hour!"

Durkin stared at her, his mouth moving as if he were chewing gum. Finally, whatever internal dialogue he had been engaged in ended and his lips closed, his eyes livid.

"You want to know what happened?" he forced himself to say. "I'll tell you what happened. Some punk kids violated the contract, that's what happened. They nearly got me killed. And not just me, this whole goddamn world too."

"How'd they do that?"

"How'd they do that? By violating the contract, that's how." Jack Durkin gripped the armrests of his chair and pulled himself up so he was sitting straight. His leathery tanned skin looked waxen as waves of indignation rolled through him. He could barely sit still he was so mad. "Those damn fool kids snuck down to Lorne Field, that's how." Hurt and embarrassed, his voice trailed off into a hoarse whisper as he added, "They threw tomatoes at me, goddamit. They threw tomatoes at me."

Lydia's jaw dropped open. She stood gaping at him, and all at once burst out laughing. She doubled over as tears of laughter streamed down her face. She almost collapsed to the floor she laughed so hard, her small bony hands holding her stomach.

"You think that's funny?"

She nodded, her body still convulsing too much for her to say anything. Durkin's lips pressed into thin bloodless lines as he watched his borderline hysterical wife. Gasping for air, she said, "You bet I find that funny. Boys throwing tomatoes at you almost killed you, huh? And that almost killed off the world? Jesus, is that funny. Thanks, I needed the laugh."

"One of them tomatoes almost knocked me off my feet."

"And that would've killed you?"

He opened his mouth, then closed it and shook his head. 'You ain't worth wasting my breath on. Now get me that bucket of hot water for my feet!"

"Get your own bucket. And there's macaroni and cheese on the stove. You can get that for yourself too."

Lydia walked out of the room laughing to herself, weaving as if she were drunk. Durkin sat fuming, too angry and tired for several minutes to do anything other than sit where he was. Gritting his teeth and with his arms shaking he pushed himself to his feet. He took a crippled, hobbling step towards the kitchen, stopped, and instead turned and headed towards the basement door, moving as if he were walking barefoot on sharp stones. A narrow wooden staircase led to an unfinished dirt basement, the ceiling low enough that he had to crouch as he moved around down there. Using a flashlight he found the two stones along the back wall that he was looking for. With a little bit of muscle he slid them out. Behind them was a wooden box that held the contract for the Caretaker of Lorne Field. Durkin brushed off his hands and took the contract out of the box. He tried to read it with his flashlight but was squinting too much and couldn't make it out. He put the box back into its hiding place and replaced the stones. Grimacing from the pain radiating through his feet, he gingerly held the vellum paper by its edges and headed back upstairs. Once he was out of the basement, he hobbled to the head of the staircase leading to the second floor and bellowed for his two boys to come downstairs. Bert emerged from the boys' bedroom and asked him what he wanted.

"Get my reading glasses from my night table drawer, and get your ass down here."

Bert nodded and disappeared into his parent's bedroom. He reappeared a minute or so later grinning stupidly and holding a pair of glasses. Before he could take a step down the stairs, Durkin stopped him, asking him if he knew where his brother was.

"Lester's watching TV."

"Tell him to get his ass down here, too!"

Bert disappeared again. Durkin heard his younger son tell Lester that he was wanted downstairs, then heard Lester complain that he was busy watching one of his shows and to tell dad he'd be down later. Durkin yelled out for Bert to tell his brother that unless he wanted to watch TV standing up and holding an icepack to his bottom he'd better do as he was told, 'cause if he had to go upstairs that'd be the only way Lester would be comfortable enough afterwards to watch anything. Even though both boys heard what was yelled, he heard Bert repeat it to Lester, then Lester complaining and bitching and moaning about it all the way to the top of the stairs. When his older boy saw him, his eyes went blank and his mouth formed into a small hurt oval. He asked what was so important.

"I want you two boys down here now," Durkin ordered brusquely. "I got something important to say to both of you."

Bert good-naturedly raced down the stairs, but Lester grumbled as he walked down them, moving as if he were as exhausted as Durkin felt. Durkin couldn't help feeling a pang of regret that the boys' births hadn't been reversed. Even though Bert was small-framed, he would've made a fine caretaker, but Durkin had his doubts whether Lester was of the proper material.

Well, the boy will just have to grow into it, Jack Durkin thought solemnly. *If he didn't, God help us all.* He moved back to the recliner and sat, trying to hide from his boys how damned tired he felt. After Bert handed him his reading glasses, Durkin told him to fetch him a bucket of hot water and Epsom salts for his feet, then directed Lester to get him a plate of macaroni and cheese and something to drink. "Afterwards you two take a seat on that sofa. I got something important to say to the both of you."

Bert raced into the kitchen. Lester continued to grumble to himself, hands shoved deep into his pants pockets. Durkin sighed to himself as he watched him. This was going to have to change. Somehow that boy was going to have to develop the right attitude. He slipped his reading glasses on and read through the contract until he found the clause he was looking for. Grimly he reread it. It was as he thought.

Bert returned first with the bucket of hot water. Durkin took his socks off, rolled up his pants and stuck his feet in it. Bert bounced onto the sofa, eager, attentive. "Dad, what's so important?" he asked.

"Wait until your brother's here," Durkin muttered without much enthusiasm. He tried to keep his expression stone-faced and hide the relief he felt soaking his sore feet. It was another five minutes before Lester emerged from the kitchen with a plate of food and a glass of water. Durkin took both from him, putting the plate on the end table next to him. The water was lukewarm. Lester couldn't bother putting an ice cube in it. And of course, he couldn't even think of bringing a fork with him from the kitchen. Without bothering to hide his disgust, Durkin ordered his son back to the kitchen for a fork. It was five minutes more before Lester returned with it. He then joined his brother on the sofa, rolled his eyes and stared sullenly at his dad. Durkin picked up the plate of food and took a few bites of it. The macaroni and cheese was tasteless. Cardboard mixed with breadcrumbs and stale cheese wouldn't have tasted much worse. He dropped the plate back onto the end table and gave his two boys a hard look.

"You boys hear of anyone sneaking down to Lorne Field today?" Durkin asked, his tone icy, dispassionate. Both boys shook their heads, both taken off-guard by his manner. "Why?" Bert asked. "What happened?"

"Never you mind."

"It looks like something happened," Lester said, recovering enough to show a smirk. "You smell like tomatoes. Looks like you got it on you, too. Your clothes, even your face and hair."

"Is that what happened?" Bert asked wide-eyed. "Did some kids sneak down there and throw tomatoes at you?"

Durkin's eyes narrowed as he studied both his boys; Lester making no effort to hide his smirk, Bert looking honestly concerned. "You two ask around," he said. "You hear anything, you tell me."

"Wow," Bert murmured. "That really happened?"

"Don't you two say nothin' to no one about it. Just ask around. See if any of your friends know about it." Durkin held up the three-hundred-year-old document he had brought up from the basement. "I never showed you boys this before, but this is the Caretaker contract. Most important document in this world."

"Big deal," Lester said under his breath.

"What was that?"

"Nothin'."

"He said 'big deal,'" Bert said.

"You bet it's a big deal," Durkin said. "You're going to be Caretaker in less than four years."

"No, I'm not," Lester argued stubbornly. "I asked mom and she says I don't have to."

"Oh yes, you do, son. It's stated so in the contract. When you turn twenty-one, you become Caretaker. That's the way it's going to be, Lester."

"Mom says I don't have to listen to you."

"That's 'cause your mom's a damn fool. This contract's the most important document in this world. You're going to honor it. You got to. There's no choice in the matter."

Lester's oval mouth contracted into a small dot as he stared blankly at the floor. Bert interjected that he could take the Caretaker job if Lester didn't want it.

Durkin smiled sadly at him. "Don't work that way, Bert. The contract clearly states the eldest son must be the Caretaker. So unless something were to happen to your brother, it just can't be done."

"Why don't you just pretend something happened to me," Lester said, his lips forming into a bitter smile.

Durkin brought his hand up to his face and squeezed his eyes. When he pulled his hand away, his eyes had reddened some. "Lester, what do you think I do all day?"

Lester looked up from the floor and stared at his dad, a hurt look playing on his mouth. He pushed out his bottom lip and said that he walked around some stupid field all day and pulled out weeds. That it was the lamest job in the world.

"That's what you think I do, huh? How about you Bert, is that what you think I do?"

Bert shrugged, smiling noncommittally.

"Those ain't weeds I pull out," Durkin said. "They're

Aukowies. I'll go over the book with the two of you later, but the only reason the world's safe is 'cause I go out there every day and pull them from that field."

Lester smirked, but he didn't say anything. Durkin couldn't help feeling hot under the collar watching his son. He held his breath, counted to ten trying to cool off. "Lester," he said, struggling hard to control his voice, "you don't think I'd rather be doing something else with my life? You think I like carrying the weight of the world on my shoulders? But it's our burden to bear, son. When you think about it, it's a great honor—"

"Yeah, such a great honor. That's why it pays you eight thousand dollars. I'd make twice that working at McDonald's."

Durkin fidgeted, turned away from his son to look out the window. "It's more than just eight thousand dollars, Lester. This home is deeded to the Caretaker and his family." He stopped for a moment to stare at the crescent moon in the sky. In the dusk a bat flew in a herky-jerky motion across it and then zigzagged out of sight. He turned slowly back to his son. "Used to be no honorarium was provided in the contract 'cause it was expected of the townsfolk in the county to provide for the Caretaker's needs. They amended the contract back in 1869 to add the honorarium. Then eight thousand dollars was a lot of money."

"It's squat now."

Durkin shrugged his stooped rounded shoulders. "Maybe so," he said, "but back in 1869 it was a lot of money. Enough for a man and his family to be well taken care of." He fidgeted more in his chair, picking at some dirt under his nails. Without much conviction, he added, "That was what was intended with the honorarium. But you're right, eight thousand dollars ain't what it used to be. When I started as Caretaker it was a good enough salary but, well, now things have to be fixed. I'm going to bring it up to the town council. They're going to have to fix it. It's only right that they do."

"Dad, what are Aukowies?" Bert asked.

"They're bogeymen," Lester said with a knowing smirk.

"No, they ain't bogeymen. Bogeymen are imaginary. Aukowies are real. I kill thousands of them every day."

"Sure you do," Lester said with another eye roll.

"You bet I do. I pull thousands of Aukowies out of that field every day. Weeds don't have a mind of their own like these things do. They don't try to cut off your fingers with razor-sharp pincers. And they sure as hell don't scream when you kill them."

"They scream?" Bert asked.

"If you listen carefully enough you can hear them. Sounds kind of like a mouse in a trap."

"Do they look like weeds?"

"When they're small maybe. But if you know what to look at you can tell they ain't no weeds. You got to remember, though, I pull them up before they get a chance to mature. A one-day-old Aukowie looks a lot different than an eight-day-old one."

"What do they look like after eight days?"

"They don't look anything like weeds then or anything else for that matter. After eight days they're ready to rip themselves free from the ground. Nine feet in length by then, big razor-sharp fangs everywhere. Bloodthirsty suckers who move like the wind. Not much anyone could do about them at that point."

"If they're not weeds, why don't you bring one home?"

Lester asked, some nervousness and uncertainty edging into his voice.

"Can't do it," Durkin said. "Contract specifies all Aukowie remains must be burnt in a stone pit on the eastern side of Lorne Field, with the ashes first mixed with lime and then buried. But I can bring you there. Let you see for yourself."

"How about me?" Bert asked.

"Sorry, son. Contract allows me to bring the eldest son to train on the killing of the Aukowies. I can't bring you, though. Not allowed by the contract."

"When are you taking me?" Lester asked.

"A few days." Durkin appraised his older son carefully. "Need to make sure you're prepared first. I got to get you a pair of good quality work boots and gloves. This ain't no fooling around. These are dangerous critters."

"I want to go too," Bert said, pouting.

Durkin sighed. "You're just going to have to be satisfied with your brother telling you about it. I got to call the town sheriff now, tell him about those delinquents violating the contract. It's serious business, and their punishment's spelled out clearly in the contract—"

"What's their punishment?" Lester asked, his voice a nervous squeak as he interrupted his dad.

"Nevermind that. But you boys ask around. You hear anything, you let me know." Durkin hesitated, his leathery features softening. "I thought it important to talk to you boys about what I do. It's important business, ain't no joke. You hear your mom talking foolishness or other kids in the town making jokes about it, just remember, they don't know any better. You boys want to go back to your TV now, go ahead. Bert, get me the phone."

Lester moved slowly off the sofa and took his time making his way up the stairs. He stopped when he got to the top. Half crouching in the shadows of the upstairs hallway, he strained to listen to his dad's phone conversation with the sheriff.

🌱

Sheriff Dan Wolcott tried to remain patient while he sat in the front seat of his Jeep and listened to Jack Durkin, his face wearing the same patient smile as if he were listening to the ranting of an elderly person suffering from dementia. After a while, though, some color tinged his angular face and before too long his large ears were burning red.

"Jack," he said, "we're not going to publicly hang some boys for throwing tomatoes at you."

"They violated the contract," Durkin argued stubbornly, his own face redder than the sheriff's. He held the contract up in front of him and pointed a thick finger at it. "It says right here anyone interfering with the Caretaker's sacred duties needs to be hung publicly for all the town to see." Durkin found the clause and read it to the sheriff for the sixth time, his voice shaking with anger.

"Jack, let's be reasonable. If you really want to make a big deal over some kids throwing tomatoes, then fine, I'll ask around, and if I can find the kids, I'll talk to their parents. Maybe see if we can arrange for them to do some of your weeding as punishment. How's that sound?"

Durkin was too furious to talk. All the color he had bled out of his face leaving it sickly white. Sheriff Wolcott watched him for a while, then shrugged. "I'm sorry some teenage boys did that to you, Jack, I truly am, but that's what teenage boys do." Wolcott paused to shake his head, his thin patronizing smile shifting back into place. "Look, why don't you go back inside your house, clean yourself off, maybe take a nice hot bath and try to relax. I'll talk to some of the teenagers around town, put a little fear in them and make sure this doesn't happen again. How's that sound?"

"You can't just turn your back on the contract," Durkin forced out, his voice harsh, barely above a whisper. "This is a sacred document. You have an obligation."

"Look, Jack, that piece of paper is a relic, a fairy tale, nothing more. Some towns have apple festivals, some have pumpkin contests, we have a quaint tradition of having a family weed a field sitting out in the middle of nowhere. Just be thankful you're being given a nice house for your family and some spending money for what you do, okay, Jack?"

"Sheriff Ed Harrison believed in what I did!"

"Yeah, well, last I heard Ed's sitting in a senior care home right now having his diapers changed a dozen times a day without a clue what planet he's on, so excuse me if I don't put much stock in what he has to think. Sorry if I'm a bit blunt, Jack, but if you're going to start talking nonsense about hanging kids in the town square, then this is what you should expect."

"Those ain't weeds I'm pulling out of that field everyday."

"Yeah?"

Flustered, Durkin took the baseball cap from his back pocket and handed it to Wolcott. "One of the Aukowies did that," he said. "After the cap was knocked off my head."

Wolcott held the cap up and examined it, running his finger along the torn fabric. "This looks pretty threadbare to me," he said. "It could've ripped open just by being hit by a tomato. At least that's how it looks to me."

"Damn it, an Aukowie sliced that open. Did it right in

front of my eyes." Anger choked him off. When he could, Durkin sputtered, "If you saw what they were you'd be treating this contract with the respect it deserves!"

"I'll tell you what, I'll stop by the field tomorrow and you can show me, okay?"

"I can't do that. It's in the contract—"

"Yeah, of course. The contract. How could I forget. Awfully convenient, that contract. Look, it's been a long day, Jack, and I have to get back to the wife and kids. I've got no problem with this quaint little tradition we have here. You want to play the part, act cantankerous and eccentric, that's fine too, but if you start acting insane we're going to have a problem. A big problem. And you demanding that some kids get hung because they threw tomatoes at you is acting insane. Goodnight, Jack."

Wolcott waited patiently for Durkin to realize there was no point in saying anything else. After Durkin left the Jeep, the sheriff drove off, honking twice as he turned the blind corner leading away from the Caretaker's cabin.

Durkin stood frozen for a long moment, his skin color not much different than the moon overhead. It was late already. Usually by this time he was asleep in bed, but with the way his stomach was grumbling and the rage he was feeling tightening his chest, he knew he'd just be lying awake all night. Instead he got into the rusted-out Chevy Nova Bill Chambers had given him brand new twenty years earlier. It took several tries before the engine turned over, then he headed towards town.

Jack Durkin sat alone at the bar at the Rusty Nail watching the baseball game on a TV set mounted on the back wall.

The owner, Charlie Harper, had brought over a cheeseburger, a plate of fries and a pint of ale, all on the house. He always treated Durkin on the house, not that Durkin ever abused the privilege, usually only stopping by once every few months. Charlie was in his seventies and was one of only a few shop owners still around town who believed in the Caretaker's importance. Charlie poured a couple of black and tans, brought them over to a table, then moved back behind the bar to keep Durkin company. He listened grimly as Durkin told him about the day he'd had.

"Those punk kids," Charlie said.

Durkin nodded, draining what was left of his pint. He waited while Charlie refilled his glass.

"That wouldn't have been tolerated when your pa was Caretaker. Or his pa before him."

"There'd be holy hell if they tried that with either of them," Durkin agreed.

Charlie shook his head, frowning. "It's just not right," he said. "Sheriff Wolcott just blew you off?"

"Yep. He thinks all I do is pull weeds all day. That my job's nothing but a joke. 'A quaint tradition' was how he put it."

Charlie's frown deepened, his large face forming into a massive crease. "That's the problem today," he said. "When I was a kid we were taught to respect what you Durkins did for us. But it's just not done these days. Parents worry too much about upsetting their precious little kiddies. Making it all into nothing but ghost stories instead. It's just not right."

"Big part of the problem's the size of the honorarium," Durkin said. "You pay someone so little, how can you respect what they do? But it didn't used to be so little." He paused to wipe some beer from his mouth and watch a groundball go up the middle putting runners on first and third. "You know what the president's salary was when the county added the honorarium?"

Charlie shrugged. "I dunno. Two hundred thousand?"

"Nope. I looked it up once. Twenty-five thousand dollars. That's all. And you had a whole country to come up with that money. The eight thousand figure was damned good in comparison, especially since you only had a small county to raise it, mostly nothing but farmers back then."

Charlie joined Durkin in watching the game. The runner on first stole second standing up.

"Pitcher's delivery's too slow," Durkin observed. "Even I could've stole that base."

Charlie nodded in agreement.

The next batter hit a two-hopper down the third base line and over the diving glove of the third baseman, scoring both runners on base. Durkin turned away from the game in disgust.

"He wasn't positioned right," he said. "He should've been guardin' the line."

"Yep."

"And he shouldn't've dove like that. If he just stayed on his feet he could've at least knocked the ball down and saved a run. I don't know what the hell they teach players today."

Charlie looked away from the TV, distracted by the sound of muted laughter coming from a corner of the bar. Sitting at a table were the two Hagerty brothers, Jasper and Darryl, both red-faced as they laughed and elbowed each other over a private joke. The Hagerty brothers were in their early thirties and worked construction. Dressed in stained tee shirts and overalls, the long greasy brownish-blond hair on both their heads looked as if it hadn't been washed in months. Jasper pointed a finger at Jack Durkin's back and laughed harder, spitting out beer as he did so. He caught Charlie's eye and elbowed his brother, signaling him with a hushing-type gesture by placing his index finger to his lips. The two Hagerty brothers struggled to keep quiet, but both burst out laughing harder than before. Charlie asked Durkin to excuse him, then walked over to Jasper and Darryl Hagerty.

"You two boys finding something amusing?" he asked.

"Nothing," Jasper giggled, his cheeks inflated as he tried to control himself. Darryl said, "We were only talking about produce. Heard of a new use for tomatoes." Both brothers sprayed beer over themselves as they exploded with laughter.

"I think you two had better leave," Charlie said.

"Aw, come on, Charlie, we're just having some fun," Jasper said, his laughter dying down to a sputter. Darryl, grinning widely, wiped tears from his face.

"I mean it. I want you to leave now. And I don't want you coming back here."

Charlie took a step towards them, his large hands balled into fists, and the humor left the Hagerty brothers' faces. The brothers were big men and less than half the age of Charlie Harper, but Charlie was also a big man with large forearms and thick bones and a face that showed scars from dozens of barroom fights. As the Hagerty brothers tried to stare him down, the violence compressing their mouths faded to something more like petulance. Darryl cracked first and shifted his eyes towards the exit. "Plenty of other places to spend my money," he said. He got up and walked towards the door. Jasper Hagerty followed him out of the Rusty Nail.

Charlie walked back behind the bar and rejoined Durkin. "Hell with them if they can't show the proper respect," he said.

Durkin kept his eyes trained on his beer. "That's what it has come to. Being laughed at by a couple of oafs like them." He seemed lost in thought for a moment, then smiled reluctantly. "It's tough enough every day looking out at a field growing full of Aukowies, knowing I got almost four years left before Lester can take over. With the way the town's acting, I just don't know, Charlie. I'm getting tired."

"What are you trying to say?"

"I don't know. Nothing."

"You're not going to stop your weeding?"

Durkin didn't answer him.

"Jesus, Jack, if you are planning that give me some notice." Charlie forced a nervous smile. "At least give me a chance to get on the first plane I can to Tahiti."

"It wouldn't do you any good. Aukowies would be there quick enough. Three or four weeks tops."

"Jack, come on, you can't let a couple of dumb asses like the Hagerty brothers get to you."

"It's not just them, Charlie. It's the whole town. Chrissakes, even my wife, my two boys."

"Your boys don't believe?"

"Maybe Bert, but Lester can't keep the smirk off his face." He smiled weakly and waved a hand in front of him as if he were waving away the last few minutes. "Don't worry, Charlie. Just feeling sorry for myself, that's all. I may be tired but I'm not quitting my weeding. Hell, only a couple of months to first frost. I'll make it. And things are going to change with Lester. I'm taking him with me in a few days. He'll see firsthand those ain't no weeds."

Charlie's heavy eyelids drooped a bit as he nodded to himself. "Any chance you can take me out there sometime?" he asked.

"I can't do that. That would be violating the contract."

"It might help to have other people see those creatures firsthand."

Durkin thought about it and shook his head. "I'd like to. But I can't violate the contract. If I start with this, who knows what rule I'd bend next. At some point we'd all be lost."

Charlie stroked his chin, considering that. "How about taking pictures of them. Anything in the contract against that?"

"Shouldn't be anything against it. Contract was written before cameras existed. Problem is, from a picture I doubt they'd look much different than a weed."

"You own a camcorder?"

Durkin shook his head.

"I'll loan you mine. I use it to take movies of my grand-kids. You film those creatures and I think people around here will change their attitude."

Durkin sat still for a long moment, then nodded slowly. "I could do that," he said. "As long as there's nothing in the contract against it. You think you could teach me how to use one of those things?"

"Sure. They're easy to learn. I should be able to teach you in a few minutes. I'll tell you what—I'll bring it over to your house tomorrow night."

Durkin sat straighter on his barstool, his shoulders barely stooped, his chest looking less caved-in than usual. It was almost as if some of the invisible weight had been rolled off his shoulders. Not all, but some. "Okay, then," he said.

Chapter 4

The next morning Lydia surprised her husband by having the boys at the table with him for breakfast and by serving fried eggs and bacon with rye bread toast and grape jelly. Jack Durkin eyed the food suspiciously, then asked his wife what got into her and why she was serving real food for a change.

"You don't like it, I can take it away and give you a bowl of corn flakes," she snapped back at him.

"No need to do that." He gave her a wary look and leaned forward, his arms circling the plate as if he were guarding it. "I was just wondering what got into you, that's all. You hit one of your scratch cards or something?"

"I don't play them! You want to keep pushing your luck, you ain't never going to see bacon and eggs again."

"Don't worry, I ain't saying another word about it." Durkin took several greedy bites, then turned to his two boys. "What do you two say? You going to thank your ma for cooking you such a nice breakfast?"

Lester was sitting across from him, his face pale, his eyes puffy and mostly shut. He grumbled something unintelligible. Bert mumbled a quick thank you. He changed the subject by asking about the Aukowies, about why they just don't cover Lorne Field with cement.

"Wouldn't work," Durkin said. "Once those suckers got big enough they'd break through. Then there'd be no stopping them."

"Where do they come from?"

Durkin soaked a piece of toast with some egg yolk and chewed it slowly while he considered the question. "I don't know," he said. "There's nothing in the Book of Aukowies about it. But my guess there's something like a root system under the field that these critters keep growing from."

Lydia let out a loud snort and mumbled something under her breath that of course there was some sort of root system, where else would weeds like that come from. Durkin turned to her, annoyed. He was about to say something when he spotted the coffee maker on the counter gurgling and brewing fresh coffee. "I thought that was broken," he said, his tone accusatory.

"I got it fixed."

The coffee finished brewing. She poured two cups and joined her family at the table, handing one of the cups to her husband. He took a slow sip and closed his eyes, savoring the flavor of the French roast. "Nice to be drinking something other than mud for a change," he said. "So why's this my lucky day? Ain't my birthday, I know that much."

"Why don't you just enjoy what you got and quit being such a damn fool," Lydia said sharply. "And quit filling your sons' heads with nonsense."

"First off, I ain't filling that boy's head with nothin'." Durkin pointed a thumb at Lester who had his eyes closed and his elbow resting on the table to support his head. "I think that boy's asleep," he added with disgust. "And even if he weren't, that head's a steel drum. Nothin' gets inside of it. As far as Bert goes, everything I'm telling him is the truth. And I'm going to prove it, too."

"How you gonna to do that?"

"You'll see," Durkin said, chuckling softly. "A couple of

days from now you'll be whistling a different tune. The whole town will be."

"You're just an old fool," she replied. "That's the only tune I'll be whistling."

"Wouldn't doubt it with all the hot air in you. But you'll see soon enough who the old fool is, you old battle—"

"Dad," Bert interrupted. "If there's a root system under that field, how about poisoning it?"

Durkin closed his mouth. For a long ten-count he kept his stare fixed on his wife, but the fresh brewed coffee and good food tempered his mood. He looked away from her to his son. "That was tried once," he told him. "My great grandpa laced the field with arsenic. According to my grandpa, the next two seasons the Aukowies came up stronger than ever."

Bert scratched his head as he thought about that. "How about digging up their root system?" he offered.

"You wouldn't want to do that. First off, no telling how deep they go. And pushing up through the ground weakens them when they're that small. You start digging a hole, you just make it easier for them so when they come up, they'll be all that much stronger. No, son, you don't want to mess with something like that. The only way to get rid of them is what we Durkins have been doing for almost three hundred years, which is weed them out when they're still small and can be handled."

Lydia started laughing to herself. A tight, cackling-type laugh. "Never mind me," she said, her small gray eyes sparkling. "When I hear nonsense like that, I can't help myself."

Durkin glared hotly at her while he used what was left of his toast to clean off his plate, then pushed himself away from the table. "You can laugh yourself sick for all I care," he said. "I save the world every day no matter what you think and I'm going to do it again today." Turning his glare towards Lester, he added, "And wake that boy up. I don't want to see good food going to waste. Especially given how little of it we get around here."

After putting on his wool socks and work boots, he stumbled towards the door and muttered a reluctant thanks to his wife for sending him out with some good food in his belly. Once he was out the door, Lydia put Lester's plate in the oven to keep the food warm, then nudged her son awake and sent him back to bed. Bert, who was a slow eater, finished his breakfast a short time later. He got up from the table, stretched lazily and told his mother he was going to go fishing at Shayes Pond and see if he could catch them lunch. Lydia watched him leave. When the door closed behind him, she went over to a cabinet where she kept a carton of cigarettes hidden, took out a pack and, after pouring herself a fresh cup of coffee, sat back at the table. She lit a cigarette, the smoke curling upward while she sat deep in thought, her face screwed into a deep frown. She had pretty much decided the night before what she was going to do, but the way her husband acted cinched it for her. He was going to prove to the world those things ain't weeds? Had he gone insane and actually believed what he was saying? It was possible he was simply putting on a show for her and Bert, but she wasn't so sure anymore. She decided it didn't matter, she was going to put an end to this nonsense. She stubbed out her cigarette and headed to the basement.

One night the previous winter she had forced an argument with her husband about the Caretaker's contract which ended up sending that old fool scurrying down to the base-

ment to prove her wrong. What he didn't know was that earlier she had Bert hide down there. Using a flashlight, she
found the two stones along the back wall that Bert had
shown her. The stones were harder to pull out than she
would've thought and for several minutes she doubted
whether she had the right ones, but eventually they budged
and, using all her muscle, she was able to work them out of
the wall. In the hole behind them was the Book of Aukowies
and a wooden box. Opening the box she found the Caretaker's contract. She knew the contract was almost three
hundred years old, but the book looked even older. Small
pieces of the leather binding flaked off when she picked it up
and the gold leaf pages inside were brittle and had aged to a
light brown. She wondered briefly how much she could sell
it for. While it wasn't in great condition, something that old
still had to be worth real money—especially since it was the
only book of its kind. Maybe an antique store would be able
to give her a price. She left the stones on the dirt floor and
carried the book and the contract back upstairs, dumping
both on the kitchen table.

She brought the phone over to the table and called Helen
Vernon and spoke quickly to her friend. While she waited
for Helen to drive over, she flipped through the pages of the
Book of Aukowies. It was the first time she had ever seen it.
The language inside was too archaic for her to make sense
of, but the book contained illustrations of Aukowies at
each stage of their development—from seedlings to full-
sized monsters. Several illustrations showed mature Aukowies
ravaging villages. Lydia's eyes dulled as she studied the
pictures.

"Nothing but a load of nonsense," she muttered to
herself.

Jack Durkin stopped to wipe his brow. Only a quarter to nine in the morning and his shirt was already damp with perspiration. He stood for a moment gazing at Lorne Field. Half of the field weeded, the other half filled with two-inch Aukowies. A breeze blew momentarily across the field and the Aukowies swayed a beat faster than the wind, trying to squeeze in the extra movement. He knew his eyes weren't playing tricks on him. He knew they were moving just that much faster than they should've been.

"Town thinks you damn things are nothing but weeds," he muttered under his breath. "They'll find out soon enough, won't they?"

The Aukowies didn't bother to answer back.

He placed his ripped baseball cap back on his head and yanked it down. A couple of safety pins held the torn fabric together enough so the cap still provided protection to his mostly bald scalp. Bending his knees and lifting, he swung the canvas sack over his shoulder and carried it to the stone pit where he dumped the Aukowie remains, then walked back to pick up his weeding where he had left off. That morning he had already come across three other Aukowies masquerading as daisies. As relentless as they were, they weren't the brightest of critters. It took them three hundred years to come up with that daisy trick, and all he could figure was it would probably take them another three hundred years to come up with their next trick—at least as long as Lester was able to grow into Caretaker material. Jack Durkin worried about that. The boy just didn't seem to have what was needed. Bert, on the other hand, would be just fine for the job. He had the right temperament for Caretaker: conscientious, resourceful, energetic. Lester wasn't any of those. But he still had close to four years to prove himself. If at that time he still seemed incapable of taking on the responsibilities of Caretaker, something would have to be done . . .

Even with the heat and humidity, even with worrying about Lester, Durkin moved with a quicker, lighter step than usual. The breakfast his wife had given him helped with his mood, but it was more the excitement of knowing there was a way to prove to the town—and more importantly to his thick-headed wife and equally ungrateful eldest son—that these weren't weeds he was pulling out all day. His situation would change after that, setting things back to the way they used to be with townsfolk recognizing the importance of what he did and with them taking care of him and his family like they used to. Like they were meant to. Which would mean Lydia would quit her shrewish nagging, and maybe he'd be able to last four more years as Caretaker without dropping dead of a massive coronary.

Durkin moved quickly as he went up and down the field pulling out Aukowies in swift, deft movements, ignoring both the crackling of his back joints when he bent over and the shrill high-pitched death cries of the Aukowies. Maybe their cries were too high-pitched for most others to hear, but he sure as hell could. And not just him. More often than not, whenever a dog was within earshot, he'd hear the thing howl as if its eardrums were being pierced. Dogs never got too close to Lorne Field, usually scampering off after their first few mournful howls. As he continued weeding, he whistled cheerfully, drowning out the dying cries of the Aukowies.

Lydia sat stiffly in the leather chair, her hands clutched tightly in her lap. Bluish veins bulged from her skeleton-thin arms like rope. Helen Vernon appeared more relaxed as she sat to her right in an identical leather chair. Across the desk from both of them sat Paul Minter, his own black leather chair plusher and more expensive-looking than theirs, which made sense since this was his office. Minter was in his early thirties, but with his Dutch-boy haircut and smooth round face, he looked like he was barely out of his teens. His brow furrowed severely as he read through the Caretaker's contract.

There were only two lawyers in town. Hank Thompson was in his seventies and had been practicing law since Lydia was a little girl. He was a kind man with a thick head of grayish hair and the bushiest eyebrows she had ever seen. A man whose gentle manner could put anyone at ease. She decided not to go to him. She didn't trust him, not with the way he acted whenever he saw her husband—deferentially, almost like he believed in this Aukowic nonsense. If she consulted him, there was no doubt in her mind that he'd run to her husband and tell him what she was planning—attorney-client privilege be damned! The other lawyer in town, Paul Minter, was a relative newcomer to the area, moving there and setting up shop only three years earlier. Lydia also had qualms about seeing him, thinking it might be best to find an attorney well outside the county, but Helen convinced her that Minter would be safe.

Minter squinted for several minutes at the contract. Finally, he placed it gently on his desk, smoothing the vellum paper out with his fingertips, a bemused expression on his face as he looked from Lydia to Helen Vernon—almost as if he were expecting one of them to admit to the prank they

were pulling on him. When both women continued to stare
vacantly back at him, he shrugged to himself and picked up
the Book of Aukowies. He took his time with it, carefully
studying each page. When he was done, he closed the book
and placed it next to the contract. He smiled in a bewildered
fashion at Lydia. "This is on the level?" he asked.

"Yep."

"This contract is dated 1710."

"That's right."

"And this book is from the same time period?"

"I'd have to think so."

"Amazing. I've been here three years and never heard a
word about any of this."

"I don't suppose you would. We usually don't talk about
it with outsiders."

"With outsiders?" He raised an eyebrow. "I guess after
three years living here I'm still considered an outsider?"

Minter waited for Lydia or Helen Vernon to contradict
him. When neither bothered to, he chuckled softly to himself. "Your husband's still weeding that field?" he asked.

"Never missed a day."

"And his ancestors have been doing it since 1710?"

"Best I know."

"This is all fascinating, but what can I help you with?"

"I need to know if that contract's legal."

"I'd have to think so."

"But how could it be? The United States didn't even exist
back then!"

"US federal courts have in the past upheld land grants
made by King George II which also predates the Declaration
of Independence," he mused. "As crazy as this contract is, I
don't see any reason why it wouldn't be valid. Of course,

there are clauses within it that violate both state law and the constitution and couldn't be legally enforced, but yes, as long as the field is weeded according to the specifications laid out in the contract, your family should be able to continue to maintain the residence granted by it. I hope that puts your mind at ease."

"No, it don't. What I want to know is if there's anything you can do to get that contract revoked."

Minter pursed his lips while he studied Lydia Durkin. "Now why would you want me to do that?"

"Because as long as that contract exists, her husband's going to keep weeding that field, leaving Lydia and her family living in poverty!" Helen Vernon volunteered.

Minter folded his hands behind his head and leaned back in his chair, the springs making a slight creaking noise. "There might be a better way to handle this," he said. "It seems to me that both you and this town are sitting on a potential goldmine."

"What do you mean?" Lydia asked.

"It's very simple. What we have here is a small, scenic New England town with a three-hundred-year-old legend of monsters growing out of the ground and a Caretaker who protects the townsfolk from them. People eat that kind of stuff up. Do you realize how much tourism Salem, Massachusetts, rakes in each year because of their history with witch trials which, by the way, didn't even occur in Salem?"

When both women continued to stare blankly at him, he smiled knowingly. "A lot of money," he said. "I'd have to think you have the same potential here." He nodded slowly to himself as he thought it over. His tongue darted past his lips, wetting them. "This could definitely work. Imagine the

Caretaker's cabin turned into a museum with an attached gift shop selling tee shirts and replicas of this book, along with plastic models of monsters and God knows what else. We could even laminate the weeds and sell them too. And that's only the tip of the iceberg. Picture tours to Lorne Field where we let people watch while your husband pulls little monsters out of the ground. Pipe in some unearthly screaming noises, along with some visual effects like monsters shooting past people's heads. This could most definitely work. This could make all of us very wealthy, Mrs. Durkin."

"How wealthy?"

"I'd have to think millions."

"Millions . . ." Helen Vernon whispered.

"Jesus," Lydia said.

Minter pulled himself forward, a sheen of excitement flushing his round face. "Mrs. Durkin," he said. "There's quite a bit of work needed to get this started. We're going to have to get approval from the town council. Also we need to line up investors and bring in the right business people. It's going to take me a few days to consult with people and draw up contracts, but we should be able to talk more about this early next week. How does all that sound?"

Lydia started to nod, then made a face as if she'd been punched in the stomach. "My damn fool husband's not going to go for this."

"Of course he will," Minter said. "I'll talk to him. Why don't we wait until I have more information and the contracts drawn up. Then I'll sit down with him. Don't worry about anything."

He shook hands with Lydia and Helen Vernon. When Lydia reached for the items she had brought, Minter asked if she could leave them with him.

"I can't do that."

Minter raised a dubious eyebrow. "Why not?"

"He'd throw a fit if he knew I'd taken those. Nobody else is supposed to know about his secret hiding place."

"I'm sure it will be okay."

"No, it won't be. I need those back. And you can't let on that I ever showed you them."

Minter opened his mouth to argue but saw it was useless. "I'll have copies made instead," he said. "Why don't you wait here. I'll let you know when they're done."

Minter gathered up the contract and book and left the room. Lydia sat back down in the chair. She looked down and saw her hands shaking. She couldn't stop them.

"I'm shaking like a leaf," she told Helen Vernon.

"I don't blame you."

"Pinch me. Make sure I'm not dreaming."

"You're not dreaming, hon."

"You think he knows what he's talking about?"

"I think so," Helen said. "It makes sense to me. If people go to Salem for witches, why not here for our monsters, even if they're nothing but a bunch of weeds? Lydia, honey, I think you're going to become rich."

"As long as my husband doesn't screw this up."

"Why would he do that?"

Lydia didn't say anything.

"Honey, I'm sure Jack's going to be as thrilled about this as you."

"You don't know how crazy he can be."

"If Jack interferes with this, you'd have every right to have him committed!"

"I'll do more than that," Lydia said, a darkness passing over her eyes. "I'll skin that old fool from head to toe."

The door to the office swung open and Minter walked back in. "My receptionist is making copies now," he informed them cheerfully. "It shouldn't be more than a few minutes."

"How much are you going to be charging for this?" Helen asked.

Minter smiled at her, but with his mouth only. "I believe that's between me and the Durkin family."

"I'm asking for her."

Minter looked from Helen to Lydia. Lydia's face was hard, rigid, something that might've been carved out of stone. Her eyes locked on his. "Nothing upfront. Just the typical fifteen percent management fee," he said.

"That sounds awfully high."

"It's not," he said. "And it's not negotiable."

"Fifteen percent's fine with me," Lydia said. "You work everything out and get my husband to go along with it, then you'll deserve it."

"Mrs. Durkin, we'll work this out. Your husband won't be a problem. Trust me."

Minter's receptionist stuck her head in and informed them that the copies were ready. Paul Minter took turns shaking hands with Lydia and Helen Vernon. When he took Lydia's hand, he covered it with both of his own. His smile appeared genuine as he gave the back of her bony hand a warm pat. "I'm very happy you came in today," he told her. "This is going to be a boon, not just to you and me, but to the whole town. I should be calling you early next week, but feel free to call me anytime before that."

On their way out, Helen told Lydia to cheer up. "Honey, you just won the lottery. No reason to be moping like this."

"I'll cheer up after my husband proves to me he ain't as big a fool as I think he is."

Later that evening when Jack Durkin returned from Lorne Field, he stumbled through the doorway, sniffed, then yelled out whether that was pot roast he was smelling.

"Take your work boots off!" Lydia yelled back from the kitchen. "I don't want you tracking dirt everywhere!"

"I'll damn well do what I want in my own home!" he yelled back to her, but he did a couple of one-legged jigs while he pulled off his work boots. With only a slight hobble to his gait he made his way to the kitchen. Lydia stood by the stove stirring something in a pot. She frowned at him. He ignored it and breathed in deeply.

"You are making pot roast," he exclaimed. "What's gotten into you, woman?"

"Shut up, you old fool," she muttered under her breath.

Durkin walked over to the stove, reached to lift the lid from a large pot that had been put on simmer. His wife slapped his hand with a sharp crack. "It'll be ready soon enough. Don't get in the way!"

Durkin brought the knuckle of his slapped hand to his mouth and sucked on it. He was in too good a mood, though, to let her usual cantankerous behavior upset him. Craning his neck so he could look over her shoulder, he saw that she had mashed potatoes in the pot she was stirring. "Yankee pot roast and mashed potatoes, huh? You find out I'm dying or something?"

"Don't let it get to your head. Lester and Bert both been asking for it."

Durkin stepped back from his wife. Her thin body was stiff as she stirred the potatoes, almost stony, but there was something close to tenderness softening the corners of her mouth. Something like that in her eyes, too.

"Hot as hell out there today," he told her. "But I was

able to get off my feet a few times. It helped. I ain't feeling so much like a cripple right now."

"So you napped on the job, huh?"

Red flashed for a moment deep in his skull—almost like a firecracker had gone off—but he swallowed back the insult he had ready for her. Something about the softness around her eyes and mouth made him.

Gotta give the old battle-axe credit, he thought, *she knows how to push my buttons better than anyone.*

"Nothing like that," he said. "Had an extra spring in my step, that's all. It must've been all that good food you served up for breakfast. Anyway, I finished all my weeding early and got to rest as much as twenty minutes at a time."

"You gonna stand there jabberin' all night?"

He shook his head. "Nope. Just had a good day, that's all."

"Why don't you make yourself useful and set the table. Dinner's almost ready."

"Make myself useful? Saving the world all day ain't making myself useful enough?" He again swallowed back the bile ready to be spat back at her. He turned away from her and muttered under his breath that he'd call the boys down to do that.

He started to leave the kitchen. Lydia reluctantly caught a glimpse of him over her shoulder. "Jack," she asked, "how you planning to prove those ain't weeds?"

He half-way faced her, a sly smile showing. "I'll tell all of you over dinner," he said. Then he left the kitchen. She heard him yell out to the boys from the hallway for them to come downstairs and help their mother.

Earlier that day when she had come back from seeing Paul Minter, Lydia sat at the kitchen table lighting up one cigarette after the next trying to calm her nerves. The reversal of fortune the attorney was offering seemed too far-fetched. Go from barely scraping by to being rich with a snap of a finger? Thinking about it, though, it made sense. People go all over for amusements. Disney World, carnivals, haunted houses, any little place that was odd and different. Why not here? And why not her? As Helen had said, it was like winning the lottery. But there was a catch. For them to cash in her husband would have to go along with it.

That thought had brought her out of her near catatonic state. She knew he wouldn't do anything that went against the contract. An impulse hit her to burn the damn thing but instead she read it carefully, line by line. And she kept going over it until she understood it.

She knew he wouldn't agree to let people come out to Lorne Field to watch him. And she knew selling those weeds would also be a sticking point for him. But the rest of it seemed possible. None of the other things violated the contract. Nothing in the contract stated that the Caretaker's Cabin couldn't be turned into a museum and gift shop. Nothing in it against selling tee shirts and dolls. As pigheaded as he was, the only thing that mattered much to him was that piece of paper. It governed his life and set the rules he lived by. Made him pretty much live like a hermit spending half the year pulling those damn weed and the other half sitting alone in their house, supposedly gathering his strength for the next season. Anything falling outside of that contract didn't concern him in the least. Once she realized he'd probably go along with most of what the lawyer wanted she started shaking worse than before, her teeth chattering as if she had a 103 degree fever. She had to grab herself and rock back and forth in her chair for a good half hour before she could stop.

For most of the rest of the afternoon she debated whether to broach the subject with him or leave it to the attorney as planned. She decided that if she brought the plan up to him he'd turn her down just to be obstinate and that it would be better to let the attorney do it later, after all the details were worked out. After settling on that, she went shopping and bought the ingredients for pot roast and mashed potatoes.

Bert entered the kitchen. He told her that it smelled good in there and that dad had asked him to help her set the table. The way Bert grinned good-naturedly at her, she couldn't help herself from hugging him and giving him a long kiss on the forehead.

"What was that for?" Bert asked.

"Nothing." She wiped a couple of tears from her eyes. "Why don't you help me set the table?"

By the time the plates and silverware were set down, Lester came into the kitchen and murmured that he was told to help. "Why don't you get the water glasses, dear." Lester made a face to indicate how cruelly he was being put upon, but trudged over to the cabinet for the glasses. Lydia asked Bert to tell his pa that dinner was ready.

The kitchen table was cramped enough with all four of them sitting around it, but with the place settings, pots and serving spoons positioned in the middle of the table, there was barely room for the salt and pepper shakers. It'd been months since they'd eaten dinner together. Durkin carefully inspected the pot roast and mashed potatoes, then told his boys to thank their ma for preparing such a nice dinner. While spooning out the food he cracked a couple of jokes at his own expense and laughed at them, too. His good mood seemed contagious, not that it took a lot to get Bert grinning.

Lester tried but couldn't keep from laughing at a few of the jokes, and even Lydia at one point cracked a smile. When Durkin, in between bites of pot roast, asked his sons if they'd found out anything about the delinquents who threw tomatoes at him, the mood shifted quickly. Forget dark clouds, more like a total eclipse had descended upon the room. Bert said he'd been asking around but no one knew anything. Lester shrugged, said he heard it was some kids from another town, but he couldn't find out anything else.

"What other town?" Durkin demanded.

"I dunno. That's all I heard."

"Who'd you hear it from?"

"I dunno. I just heard some kid say it."

"Well, come on, boy, think. What was the name of this kid?"

"I dunno. Just some kid. I wasn't paying attention."

"For Chrissakes, start paying attention to what's going on around you!" Exasperated, Durkin pointed his fork at Lester for emphasis. "You keep asking around. And get me the name of that boy. This is important."

"Maybe you should let it drop," Lydia said.

Durkin stared hard at her. He could've been choking with the way his face purpled. A minute passed before he moved. All the while Lydia ignored him and casually ate her dinner.

"I'm not going to let this drop," he said finally.

"Then don't. Go ahead, give yourself a stroke worrying about it."

"They violated the contract!"

"I think I heard something about that already."

Durkin flashed her an annoyed look before turning to his boys and telling them to keep asking around. "I want to know their names and what town they came from," he said.

He pushed his plate away and stared petulantly at it. Bert made a face like he had an upset stomach. Lester started pushing his food slowly around his plate. Lydia watched all this for a while, then asked her husband whether he was going to let good food go to waste.

"I lost my appetite."

"That's too bad. Especially since it's your favorite."

Durkin stared reluctantly back at his plate, then started eating again, slower, grudgingly. Both his sons picked up their forks and started eating again, also somewhat grudgingly.

Lydia asked her husband how he was going to prove he was pulling out something other than weeds from Lorne Field.

He waited until he finished chewing a mouthful of food and said, "I'm gonna videotape the Aukowies."

"What do you mean?"

"Charlie Harper's stopping by later tonight to drop off a video camcorder. Tomorrow I'm going to record those mean little suckers in action. There'll be no doubt then they ain't weeds."

Lydia sat still for a moment before his words made sense. Then she felt a dull throbbing start behind her eyeballs. It probably didn't matter that he was going to make a video proving those things were nothing but weeds. With or without that video, who'd actually believe they were anything but weeds? Still, realizing that didn't stop the dull throbbing behind her eyeballs. She couldn't stop thinking that somehow he was going to screw things up. That somehow his video would ruin the mystique of monsters growing in Lorne Field. That it would send that lawyer's plans flushing down the toilet and their future along with it. She was going to have to call Paul Minter tomorrow and tell him about it. Thinking about that made the dull throbbing worse. She closed her eyes and rubbed small circles along her temples.

"Maybe you can wait until next week," she whispered.

"What did you say? Speak up, I couldn't hear a word you said."

"I said maybe you could wait to do that."

"What for? The quicker I prove to you and the rest of the town what these Aukowies really are, the better." He turned to point a forkful of food at Lester. "Which reminds me," he said. "I need you to go to the Army Surplus store on Maple tomorrow morning. Talk to Jerry Hallwell. He knows what you need and it's already taken care of. After that I want you heading straight to Lorne Field. Don't enter it, though. Don't even step a foot in it. I'll meet you at the edge."

"Aw, geez," Lester complained. "I have plans for tomorrow—"

"Why you asking Lester to go there?" Lydia interrupted, her voice sounding awkward to her, almost as if it were coming out of an echo chamber.

"'Cause it's about time I teach him how to kill Aukowies. And besides, I need him to help me make my video." He turned to Lester, "About your plans. Too bad. We all got sacrifices we need to make. You just do as you're told."

"Dad, if you want I could do it instead," Bert volunteered.

"I wish I could let you." Durkin sighed, then shared a wicked grin with his son. "Bert, you should've seen the

Aukowies today when I set fire to them. I don't know why, but the flames shot twenty feet upwards. It was something to see."

"Aww," Bert said. "I wish I could've seen that."

"Well, you will. That's going to be one of the things I plan on taking video of. Although I ain't never seen flames shoot that high from them before. Don't know whether the Aukowies will cooperate like that tomorrow, but we'll see."

"It would be better if you wait on this," Lydia said.

Durkin ignored her and took a second helping of pot roast.

Lydia sat thinking. The din of forks scraping plates and water glasses clinking and the grunting and chewing noises from her husband and sons blended with the roaring of blood rushing through her head. That fool husband of hers would probably try to give his video to the local news stations, not only killing that lawyer's plans but making the family an even bigger joke to the town than they already were. She knew she'd have to make sure no one saw any video he took. She'd still talk with Paul Minter the following day, but no matter what, she was going to have to make sure no one saw any of that fool's video.

The certainty calmed the roaring inside her head. The din became distinct noises again. The throbbing behind her eyeballs eased to a dull headache. She opened her eyes and continued eating her dinner. She was finishing up when there was a knock on the door. Durkin got up from the table and, after a minute or so of talking with someone outside the house, brought Charlie Harper into the kitchen. Charlie carried a six-pack of imported beer in one hand and a video camcorder in the other. He put the six-pack in the refrigerator before joining her husband at the table.

"Thought you could use some good beer," he said.

"I appreciate it, Charlie. How about joining us for some pot roast?" Durkin offered. "Lydia really outdid herself this time."

"Smells great, but I better not." Charlie showed an uncomfortable grimace as he looked around the room. He said to Lydia, "Ah, Mrs. Durkin, I apologize for interrupting your dinner. I didn't know what time you and Jack go to bed and I didn't want to risk waking you folks up."

She murmured something about it being alright.

Charlie nodded, mussed up Bert's hair. "Damn, if you're not growing like a string bean," he said. "Last time I saw you, you were half this tall." Bert grinned sheepishly and said something innocuous before turning back to his food.

"And it's a pleasure seeing the future Caretaker," Charlie said to Lester, his hand outstretched to him. Lester looked annoyed, but reached up and offered a weak handshake in return. "Not me," he said. "Pulling weeds all day is lame."

"What's he talking about?" Charlie asked Durkin, his heavy face showing alarm.

"Don't mind him. He's going to be Caretaker when he turns twenty-one. As the contract requires."

"No, I won't!"

"Oh, yes you will, Lester. When you see what's at stake you'll change your tune fast enough." Durkin's eyes narrowed as he stared at his son. "And I want you to join us. Mr. Harper's going to teach me how to use his camcorder and I want you to learn, too."

"I already know how to use one. I'm not an idiot."

"Don't you dare talk to me like that. And you're going to join us."

"I'm still eating—"

"I said now!"

Charlie cleared his throat and said, "Jack, that's all right. I don't mind waiting."

"No, you come all the way here to do me a favor, I'm not having you wait. And you told me at the door Sam's minding the bar for you. You've been put out enough."

"Jack, really, it's not a problem. A few more minutes won't matter and Sam's fine behind the bar."

Durkin shook his head. "Right now that old codger's probably drinking you blind."

Lydia, her voice pinched, suggested that her husband have Charlie show him and Lester right there in the kitchen how to use his camcorder.

"I could do that," Charlie said.

Durkin's lips curled over his teeth like he wanted to argue with his wife, but he nodded. "Alright, whatever's easier for you. Lester, you get over here so you can watch."

"I can watch where I'm sitting."

"Look, I'm not going to tell you twice—"

"I have to think the boy's fine where he is," Charlie agreed. He nudged Durkin good-naturedly with his elbow. "Here, let me show you how to use this." He went through the basics with Durkin, turning on the camcorder, recording video and playing it back on the view screen. He handed the camcorder to Durkin and helped him as Durkin's thick fingers moved awkwardly over the controls. After a few tries and repeated instructions from Charlie, Durkin seemed to get the hang of it.

"Okay, let me show you how to zoom."

Charlie showed Jack Durkin how to use the controls to bring the lens in and out. He had trouble manipulating the buttons with his thick callused fingers, but after a while he figured out how to position his nail just right so he could do it. He turned to Lester and asked whether he got all that.

"Hand me the camera and I'll show you."

Durkin handed the camcorder to his son, who then flicked a piece of carrot from his plate at his brother and recorded Bert's reaction as the younger boy brushed the carrot piece frantically from his hair. Lester played the video back on the view screen, all the while smirking to himself.

"Very funny," Durkin said.

"You wanted to know whether I knew how to use it."

Charlie took the camcorder from Lester and got Durkin's attention. "Let me rewind the tape. I recharged the batteries last night so you should be all set to go tomorrow." Charlie turned the camcorder off and handed it to Durkin. "You're going to let me see the video you take?"

Jack Durkin nodded. "You and the whole town."

❧

After Charlie Harper left, Jack Durkin took a couple of bottles of imported beer to the living room so he could drink them while he soaked his feet. Lydia stayed in the kitchen washing dishes and cleaning up. Both boys went upstairs. When they were alone in their room, Lester reared back with a clenched fist and struck Bert square in the shoulder.

"Oww!" Bert cried. He shied away and rubbed his shoulder, tears flooding his eyes. "Why'd you do that?"

"For being such a kiss-ass. *Oh, daddy, please let me do it instead of Lester.*" He clenched his fist tigher, muttered "asshole" under his breath.

"You better not hit me again."

"Oh, no?" Lester raised his fist to deliver another blow but Bert stood his ground. "You better not," Bert said, his voice changing to something threatening enough to stop Lester from following through with his punch. "I lied to Dad downstairs. I know you were one of the boys who threw tomatoes at him. You, Tony Morelli, Sam Parsons and Carl Ashworth."

"Bullshit." Lester's color paled. He edged closer to his brother, his mouth pushed into a tiny circle and a sour breath came out of him. "Whoever told you that is full of shit."

"Nope." Bert shook his head. "I know it for a fact. Why'd you want to throw tomatoes at Dad?"

Lester's eyes shifted away from Bert. He shook his head. He couldn't articulate to his brother the frustration and humiliation that drove him to do what he did.

"You don't want to tell me, don't," Bert said. "But you better be nice to me 'cause I know what will happen if Dad finds out what you did. I know because I snuck down to the basement this afternoon and read his contract. Want to know what will happen to you?"

Bert made a fist with his left hand and yanked it up while his head drooped towards his right shoulder, all the while his eyes bulging in a lifeless stare and his tongue pushing out of his mouth. He held that pose for a few seconds, then broke out laughing.

A red blush replaced the dead whiteness in Lester's cheeks. "You're making that up," he said.

"Nope. According to Dad's contract you're supposed to be publicly hanged for what you did."

Lester stood silently for a long ten-count. He edged several inches closer to his brother. "You're lying. I don't believe you know where his contract's hidden."

Bert shrugged and showed his boyish grin. "Don't

believe me," he said. "But you better start being nice to me. Else I'm telling Dad."

"You do and you're dead."

"No, not me," Bert said with the utmost sincerity. "But you will be. Hung by the neck." He again acted out being hung, then punched Lester as hard as he could in the shoulder.

Chapter 5

Jack Durkin wiped his brow, squinting towards Lorne Woods. Lester should've been at the field an hour ago. Durkin had already finished one pass of his weeding and was a third of the way into his second pass. *How long does it frickin' take to pick up a pair of work boots and gloves and ride your bike three miles? Can't the boy be counted on for nothin'?*

As he peered towards the woods and searched for any sign of his son, Durkin felt a sharp pain slice through his groin—almost as if someone had stuck a hand inside him and grabbed his guts and squeezed. The pain immobilized him. Sweat poured from his face, and he knew it was far more from nervousness than the heat and humidity—and he had a damn good reason for being nervous. In a corner of the field he had let an Aukowie grow to almost a foot in height. It was a violation of the Caretaker's contract to purposely let that happen, but he couldn't help it—he needed one that big so he could prove that these things weren't weeds.

The pain cutting through his groin subsided and his stomach muscles unclenched to the point where he could breathe normally again. He looked over his shoulder and stared at the foot-high Aukowie and knew it was staring right back. At that size he could make out its face clearly. Others might confuse it for leaves and branches and thorns, but to him there was no mistaking its narrow slanted eyes and evilly grinning mouth. Those so-called thorns were sharp enough to cut a man's hand off, and they'd get a lot sharper before the thing was done growing.

Durkin looked away from the foot-high Aukowie and went back to his weeding, moving slowly as he bent over and pulled out small two-inch baby Aukowies. After he had pulled out a couple a dozen of them, he sneaked a peek at the larger Aukowie. He knew it was studying him. He knew it hated him for what he was doing to its brethren. Not that hate much mattered to Aukowies. Fully matured they were killing machines that would lay waste to every human, animal, bird, fish and growth of vegetation on the planet. When they were done there would be nothing but dust and rubble left behind. With their evil grinning faces he couldn't help thinking of them as devil spawn, hatched from hell to bring about their apocalyptic ending. But of course, he knew that was nonsense. For him to believe there was truly a hell he'd also have to believe there was a heaven, and even more difficult to accept, that there was a God. How could any God put the fate of the world on one man's shoulders? How in the world could he believe in a God that would curse a family with that kind of burden? No, as much as they looked the part, he knew the Aukowies weren't born in hell. Most likely they came from another planet, maybe an asteroid that crashed hundreds of years ago, or maybe they were simply the result of the evolutionary process run amok. But heaven and hell had nothing to do with these Aukowies. They were something random, and there was no divine intervention protecting man from them. That fate fell on the Durkins and their solid but all too human shoulders. And the load seemed to be getting heavier every day.

He forced himself to keep weeding, but every so often he

had to look over at the foot-high Aukowie. He knew every minute it was growing just that much larger and knowing that made him feel funny inside. Made his legs sort of rubbery too. But there was nothing he could do about it. He needed to videotape that foot-high Aukowie in action, and in order for him to do that, he needed Lester's help. Still, every time he looked at it he had to fight back the urge to dig it up while he knew he still could.

He got careless with his weeding, too distracted by the ever-growing foot-high Aukowie to concentrate properly on what he was doing, and ended up slashed right above his glove. He wrapped a handkerchief around the wound and cursed Lester bitterly. Cursed him first for not being there on time, cursed him for his laziness, and finally for not being stillborn like his sisters before him—because if he were, then Bert would be the eldest son and would be in line to be the next Caretaker. If Bert were going to be Caretaker, he wouldn't have to worry about the human race coming to an end after Lester's twenty-first birthday.

Durkin finished tying the handkerchief around his wound. A thin red line expanded slowly across it. He couldn't afford to let any blood drip near the Aukowies—human blood drove them wild. He took his glove off and shoved it in one pocket and stuck his hand deep in the other pocket, then continued his weeding one-handed.

About the time he was halfway done weeding the field he spotted Lester trudging out of Lorne Woods. The boy moved in a slow, disinterested gait, every few feet kicking at the ground. Jack Durkin could see he didn't have his work boots or his gloves with him.

"What are you doing?" he yelled.

Lester looked up, shrugged.

"How come you don't have your boots or gloves with you? Don't tell me you dropped them off at home?"

"I dunno. I guess I forgot about them."

"You're telling me you didn't go to the Army Surplus store this morning?"

Lester shrugged again.

"For Chrissakes, I ask you to do one thing—" Durkin's eyes grew wide as he watched Lester reach down towards an Aukowie seedling growing on the edge of the field. "Damn it, Lester, get your hand away from that!" he ordered.

Lester slowly pulled his hand back, a hurt look showing on his mouth. "I just wanted to see what the big deal is about these weeds," he said.

"You want to lose a finger? That's what's going to happen if you try touching one of them without a glove."

"I'm not going to lose a finger," Lester insisted, his face a mask of hurt.

"You sure as hell will if you put your hand down there without knowing what you're doing. Just stay right where you are. I'll come get you."

Durkin heaved the canvas sack over his shoulder and started towards his son. When he got within a few feet of the boy he slung the sack to him. The weight of the sack almost knocked Lester over. "You carry that," Durkin told him. "We'll dump this first and then get started with what we need to do."

"This is heavy," Lester complained.

"You'll get used to it. Put it over your shoulder. It will be too hard carrying it two-handed like that."

Lester struggled to get the sack over his shoulder, his knees buckling. "We're taking it over to that stone pit over there," Durkin said, pointing out with a thick knobby finger where his son had to bring the sack. As he led the way, he looked back once and couldn't help grimacing watching Lester's thin bird-like legs shake as he struggled to carry the sack of dead Aukowies. He regretted thinking the things he did earlier. The boy may not be much but at least he was out there trying. As thin and slight as he was, he was going to have a hard road ahead of him as Caretaker. The Durkins historically were of a stockier build. Lester, unfortunately, had to take after Lydia's side of the family and end up as thin as a stick. The boy was already over six feet tall and didn't weigh more than a hundred and thirty pounds. When they reached the stone pit, he helped Lester dump the sack out.

"It smells bad," Lester said, wrinkling his nose.

Jack Durkin nodded. "Yep. Those dead Aukowies been baking in the sun for a few hours now, getting nice and ripe. Wait till you catch a whiff of them when I set that pile on fire later. The smell alone will prove that these ain't no weeds."

"They look like weeds," Lester said stubbornly, his eyes squinting and peering off at the field.

"You'll think differently soon. Now grab that empty sack and follow me."

Jack Durkin led the way back to the shed near the entrance of the field. "Your great great grandpa built this almost a hundred years ago," he proudly told his son. "Solid pine. Probably be around another hundred years."

Lester shrugged, didn't seem too impressed. "How come one of the weeds is bigger than the others?" he asked.

"'Cause I needed to let one get that size." Durkin stopped to wipe some sweat from his brow. He frowned deeply at the foot-tall Aukowie. "Son, you're going to have to be extra careful around that one. When they get that big they can whip out at you like a rattlesnake, and trust me, they're far more deadly than any snake."

"Sure they are," Lester muttered under his breath.

Durkin heard the crack, but showed nothing except weariness, and maybe a bit of tenderness, in his heavily-lined leathered face. "It's true," he said. "You'll be seeing soon enough, son. When they get to two feet, they get much bolder. Then they're like a rabid pit bull, flying all over the place trying to get at you. But at one foot they're still dangerous enough. Hell, even at two-inches they can hurt you pretty bad." He breathed in deeply and sighed. "Just keep your distance from that sucker when we go over to it."

"Why are we going over to it?"

"So you can record it when I dig it out. You'll see what an Aukowie really is then."

Durkin opened the door to the shed and took out a spade for Lester to hold onto. He was going to need that spade later when it came time to subdue the foot-high Aukowie. He next retrieved Charlie Harper's video camcorder that he had left in the shed for safekeeping. He struggled for a moment to hit the power button with his thick index finger, then handed the camcorder to his son. "You remember from last night how to use this, right?" he asked.

Lester rolled his eyes. "Yeah, I remember."

Durkin ignored the insolence and said, "Since you didn't wear work boots we need to stay off the field where they're growing more than an inch, otherwise they'd slice your feet to ribbons. Follow me and don't put your hands anywhere near one of them, okay?"

"Okay," Lester muttered. He hesitated and asked, "How come you've been keeping your hand in your pocket?"

"I got careless earlier." Durkin took his hand out and showed Lester the blood-stained handkerchief tied a few inches above his wrist. "You can never let an Aukowie taste human blood. Not even a drop. Don't matter how big they are, they'll go nuts if they do." He studied his own arm and nodded slowly. "Looks like I don't need to worry about bleeding on them anymore. Be careful, okay, son? You might think this is all one big joke right now, but it ain't."

Durkin untied the handkerchief from his arm and folded it back in his pocket. Blood had scabbed over his wound. He took his glove from his pocket, put it back on, then led the way along the edge of the field. When he got to where he had stopped his weeding, he told Lester to stand still.

"I was hoping today to start teaching you how to kill these things, but I can't do it without you wearing gloves. These critters are tricky. You got to grab them just the right way and pull up at just the right angle. After a while you'll get the hang of it. For now, though, watch me. Also, take a deep breath and listen carefully."

Durkin waited until his son did as he was told, then he reached down and pulled a two-inch Aukowie from the ground. He turned his head sideways to look at his son.

"You hear that?" he asked.

"Hear what?"

"The scream it made when I killed it."

"Nope. I didn't hear nuthin'."

Durkin's eyes and mouth weakened with disappointment. "You will eventually, son. Sometimes it takes practice. My pa told me it took him over a year before he started hearing it. Me, I started hearing it from the very first Aukowie I killed."

"I dunno. I didn't hear nuthin'."

"It will just take some time." Durkin straightened up and grimaced painfully as he worked a few kinks from his

back. "We're going to go over to that large one over there,"
he said. "They're longer than they look, so be careful." He
paused, smiling wistfully. "Can you see the face on it?" he
asked.

"Nope."

Durkin pointed out its eyes and mouth and horns. "You
can't see all that?"

"All I see are a bunch of leaves and vines." Lester narrowed his eyes. "Maybe some thorns, too, but that's all
I see."

"Sometimes it just takes a while, that's all," Durkin said
with a heavy sigh. "You keep looking and you'll see it."

"Dad," Lester said, "do you really believe all this?"

"What?"

"That these aren't just weeds?"

"What have I been saying?"

Lester scratched his jaw, then scratched behind his ear. "I
dunno. That's all part of the act, right?"

"Son, you'll be finding out soon this is no act." Jack
Durkin emptied out a lungful of air and sighed heavily.
"Hand me that spade. And get ready with the camera."

Lydia called Paul Minter's office at nine o'clock and was
told by his receptionist that he was in court and wouldn't be
back until after one. From that point on she sat at the
kitchen table chain-smoking through half a dozen packs of
cigarettes, all the while keeping one eye on the clock over the
oven. At one o'clock she thought about calling again but
held back. When the phone eventually rang it jolted her.

"Dorothy told me you called?" Paul Minter said.

"It's one thirty-five. She told me you'd be back by one."

"Things took longer than expected. What's up?"

Lydia told him about her husband planning to make a videotape of the weeds. How he was planning to show it to the town.

Minter took the news quietly and finally asked, "Why does he want to do that?"

"Because he wants to prove to everyone that these things ain't weeds."

"You're kidding."

"I wish I was."

Another long silence from Minter's end, then, "I don't think this would be the best thing for us."

"I didn't think so either."

"Who is your husband planning to show his videotape to?"

"Probably the local news station."

Minter digested that and said, "No, that definitely would not be good for us." Lydia could hear him coughing at his end, then spit something into a trashcan. When he came back, he asked, "Your husband doesn't actually believe what's in the book you showed me?"

"I think that damn fool believes every word of it."

"This really isn't good at all," he said softly. He cleared his throat some more. "It's one thing to have this quaint little fairy tale that everybody knows is only a fairy tale, it's quite another to rub everybody's nose in that fact . . ." He hesitated for a long moment. When he continued his voice was more controlled. "Did you tell your husband about our plans?"

"Of course not. You told me you'd talk to him after your plans were worked out."

"That's right, I did. How about if I meet with him later

today. Do you think you can bring him over to the office this afternoon?"

"He'll be at that field until eight tonight."

"Can you get him to leave early?"

"Not a snowball's chance."

"How about if I stop by your house tonight?"

"Fine with me."

"What time does your family have dinner?"

"When my husband comes home. Eight o'clock usually. We should be done by nine."

"Expect me there at nine. I'll have a talk with your husband then, and I'm sure he'll be as excited about our plans as we are."

"We'll see," Lydia said, without much enthusiasm.

"And, Mrs. Durkin, it's not just us. I've had preliminary talks with several members of the town council. There's a lot of excitement brewing over these plans. I'll be meeting with potential business partners tomorrow. But it would be best if you can keep him from showing videotapes he may have made to anyone, especially to the media, at least until I have a chance to talk with him."

"He won't be showing anyone videotapes," Lydia promised. "At least not today."

Paul Minter told her that was good news. He put his receptionist on the line to get driving directions to her cabin. After Lydia got off the phone, she chain-smoked through half a pack of cigarettes, then put on a fresh pot of coffee. While she waited for the coffee to brew, she heard some noises from outside. It sounded like a sick dog howling off in the distance. She looked out the kitchen window and saw her husband and Lester maybe a hundred yards away. Her husband had his arm around Lester's waist and seemed to be half dragging and half carrying him. Her son was shirtless and looked white as a sheet. It also looked like he was dragging something with his right hand. As they got closer she could see him more clearly. His face was screwed up as if he were dying and a redness around his eyes stood out in stark contrast to the unnatural paleness of the rest of his skin, almost as if paint had been used. She could also see he wasn't dragging anything in his right hand—that instead his shirt had been wrapped around it. She remembered him leaving the house in a green tee shirt. What was around his hand looked like it had been dyed red. She could hear him whimpering.

Lydia stood frozen as her son and husband moved closer, trying to make some sense out of the scene. Then she sprang to life and rushed out the kitchen door to meet them.

"It wasn't my fault," Jack Durkin told her.

Lydia brought Lester's head to her shoulder. His eyes were squeezed tight. What looked like paint was blood that had been smeared across his face. As she whispered to him, his mouth opened wide and he whimpered like a wounded dog. Thick strands of saliva dripped from his mouth onto her blouse. She rubbed her hand across his face wiping off tears, then started kissing his cheek, his eyes, his forehead, all the while telling him that everything was going to be okay.

Her husband repeated that it wasn't his fault. "It happened so fast," he said flatly, his expression vacant. "I didn't know what was happening until it was over."

She looked away from her son to her husband, her small eyes enflamed. "What did you do to my son?" she demanded, her voice shaking.

"Nothin'." Durkin shook his head. "I didn't do nothin'. It wasn't my fault."

Lester let loose a low cry. She gently took his hand and unwrapped the shirt that had been tied around it. Underneath was a bloody mess. She saw that his thumb was missing.

"It wasn't my fault," her husband insisted. "He was supposed to film me while I dug up one of the Aukowies. I heard something, looked over and saw he dropped the camera. Before I could stop him he reached down for it."

"You monster," she said to him, her voice still shaking and barely a whisper.

Durkin flinched. "There was nothing I could do," he said.

She flew at him, beating him over and over again in the chest, her hands clenched into tiny fists that were no bigger than small Cortland apples. Durkin stood helplessly and took it.

"There was nothin' I could do to stop it."

"Where's his thumb?" she cried. Tears streamed down her raisin-like face. "What did you do with it!"

"It's gone."

"What do you mean it's gone?"

"The Aukowies got it," he said.

"You bastard!"

"There was nothin' I could do. They took his thumb. Next thing it was gone. Nothin' left but a pink mist."

She flashed him a look mixed with hate and disgust and utter contempt, then led Lester away from him.

"You better take him to the hospital," he said, acting as if Lydia were still listening to him. "I can't. I have to go back. I have to finish weeding." There was a desperate pleading in his eyes. He waited for her to look back at him. She didn't. He wiped the back of his hand across his brow, then under his nose. "Lydia, there was nothin' I could do."

"Go to hell." She guided Lester into the passenger seat of their car and secured the seatbelt around him. She stopped for a moment to kiss him on the cheek and forehead, then got behind the wheel. She floored the gas, revving the engine to a high pitch. Durkin stood staring helplessly. He didn't bother to move when she backed the car out at full throttle, coming within a hair's breadth of clipping him.

"There was nothing I could do," he repeated to no one. He stood and watched the car race down the dirt road and saw it barely miss spinning into a tree before Lydia regained control of the wheel. When it was out of sight, he turned and headed back to Lorne Field.

The nearest hospital was two towns over in Eastham. When Lydia arrived there with Lester, the doctor handling the emergency room gave her a funny look when he saw Lester's hand. He wanted to get Lester into surgery, but before that he had questions for her. The first one was where was the thumb. All she could do was tell him she didn't know.

He was checking Lester's vital signs while a nurse attached an IV and another wrapped gauze around Lester's hand. She recognized the nurse attaching the IV as Abby Huffman's girl. She had never seen the doctor or other nurse before, knew they weren't from her town. The doctor asked how the injury happened.

"I don't know. My husband says it was an accident. That's all he told me."

"He was with your son at the time?"

"Yes."

"Anyone else with them?"

"Nope, just Lester and my husband."

"What happened to the thumb?"

"All he said was it was lost. Anyway, I don't have it and I don't know where it is."

"That's too bad," the doctor said. "It looks like a clean cut. The thumb probably could've been reattached."

"I I-how do you think it was cut off?"

"A knife."

Lester was sedated when he was brought in. He started moaning. Abby Huffman's girl told the doctor that the IV was in. He told Lydia that they were taking Lester to surgery. That not only did they need to operate on his hand, but his blood pressure was dangerously low and he needed a transfusion as quickly as possible. He looked away from her and told her that she would be escorted to a waiting area.

"I want to be with my son."

He turned only partly to face her. He was a lean man in his early thirties with a face like a razor. The look he gave her had about as much warmth as a sheet of ice.

"We have certain rules we need to follow for cases like this," he said.

"Cases like what?"

He ignored her, nodding instead to two orderlies standing nearby. They took hold of the gurney Lester was on and started wheeling it away. The doctor followed them. When Lydia tried to follow, the nurse that she didn't know stepped in her way.

"I'm sorry," the nurse said, "but I need to bring you to one of our waiting rooms."

The nurse was a good forty pounds heavier than Lydia and had a thick neck for a woman. Her forearms were also thicker than Lydia's thighs. Lydia felt very tired at that moment. Weak also. She nodded and followed the nurse to a small room that had only a table and two chairs in it. The nurse asked Lydia whether she could get her a magazine. Lydia shook her head, sat down and started to cry. She didn't want to cry in front of this other woman but couldn't help herself. She heard the door close as the nurse left.

While she waited, a woman from the hospital came to ask her questions. She was about Lydia's age but looked much younger. She wore a turtleneck sweater and a long wool skirt, which seemed to Lydia like an odd choice for the summer. Most of her questions were about their family life. It was a blur to Lydia. She was only half-aware of her answers. A short time after the woman left, two local police officers came in to talk to her. They didn't have many questions, mostly the same ones the doctor had, and a few about her husband. It was also like a blur with them. It seemed as if they were only there for seconds before they were gone. She knew it was longer, but that's what it seemed like.

When Sheriff Wolcott walked into the room she was surprised to see that it was already a quarter to five. He looked ill at ease as he sat across from her, his skin color not quite right.

"Mrs. Durkin," he said.

"Daniel."

"I understand there was an accident?"

"Yes." She looked again at her watch and slowly made sense of the fact that she'd been sitting there over two hours. "My boy should be done with surgery by now," she said, her face crumbling as she expected the worst.

"I understand the surgery went well. A doctor will be in here soon to talk to you about it, but I understand it went well and Lester's recuperating right now."

"Thank God." She started crying then, her sobs wracking her nearly skeletal frame. "Oh thank God for that."

Through the sobbing she could see Wolcott studying her, his eyes queasy and his lips turned up into a forced look of sympathy. He looked like he wanted to bolt. She sniffed a few times, got control of her crying and wiped a hand across her eyes.

"Why ain't I allowed to be with my son right now?"

"You will be," he said. He looked down at his hands, didn't seem to know what to do with them, and ended up folding them in front of him with his fingers interlaced. "I understand Lester's still in post-op, but you'll be able to see him soon. I have some questions for you."

"Well, why don't you get around to asking them!"

He smiled weakly at her then, reminding her of the way he was when he was five and she used to babysit him. The smile faded quickly. "I need to know about the accident, Mrs. Durkin."

"There's nothing I can tell you," she said. "You're going to have to ask Lester or my damned fool husband about it."

"I plan to," he said. His manner shifted momentarily to something more formal, more police-like. When he met Lydia's stare, the hardness about his face faded. "I was hoping you might have some idea what happened."

"Nope. I wasn't there."

"The doctor I spoke to thinks Lester's thumb was cut off with a knife."

Lydia didn't say anything. Wolcott tried to meet her eyes, but instead lowered his gaze back to his folded hands. "Do you think Jack might've done something like that?" he asked.

"All I know is he told me it was an accident."

"But you know him as well as anyone. Could he do something like that?"

She laughed. "Know him as well as anyone? Ha! I don't have a clue what goes on in that block of cement he calls a head. But no, he wouldn't intentionally hurt Lester. He never once laid a hand on me or the boys. It's not in him to do something like that. He makes a lot of noise but that's all it is."

"He does seem to have quite a temper."

"Not really. His bark's worse than his bite."

"What about his mental state?"

Lydia laughed again. "He's no crazier now than he's ever been."

"I don't know," Wolcott said. "I was talking to him just last night and he acted pretty crazy to me. You know that a bunch of boys snuck down to Lorne Field and threw tomatoes at him? He wanted me to track them down so he could have them hung publicly in the town square."

She shrugged. "That's what's written in his contract."

"I don't care what's in his contract, that's insane!"

"Don't yell at me, Daniel."

He nodded, contrite. "I'm sorry, Mrs. Durkin. But you have to admit someone wanting to have teenagers executed for throwing tomatoes at him is pretty insane." He waited for her to say something. When she didn't, he wet his lips and edged closer to her. He asked, "I was wondering if that contract has anything in it about cutting off someone's thumb. You know, as a punishment?"

Lydia shook her head. "I've read it. There's nothing like that in it. And my fool husband only does what's spelled out in his contract."

"I'd like to read it also."

"You come over to the house when he's not home and I'll get it for you. You just can't let him know I did it."

He licked his lips again and asked, "So you don't think Jack's acting any crazier these days than usual?"

"Nope. No more than usual."

"Then what do you think happened?"

"I have no idea. Probably it's just an accident like Jack said. He was probably showing Lester how to pull out one of those weeds, and maybe what he was using slipped. Maybe he uses a knife. I don't know. You'll have to ask him."

"I will when I talk to Jack later. Did he bring Lester back to your house after the incident?"

She nodded.

"Why didn't he come with you to the hospital?"

A dark film fell over her eyes. "He had his weeding to do."

"So he went back to Lorne Field afterwards?"

"That's right. After he brought Lester home he headed back there." She paused as she considered this, and as she did, her features weakened, becoming more like bone china than stone. "That would've been a violation of his contract. He's not supposed to leave that field until his weeding's done. It must've been difficult for him to do that." A tear leaked from her eye. She wiped it away with a hand. "When do you plan on talking to him?"

"As soon as possible."

"Daniel, can you wait until he leaves that field?"

"I don't know if I can do that—"

"It would be hard on him to have someone come by that field like that. Please, Daniel, wait until he finishes his weeding."

He started to tell her that that wouldn't be possible, that there was possible evidence at the field which he needed to examine, but instead he looked away from her and stared out the window. "I'll try, but I can't promise anything." A red-tailed hawk flew into view, and he watched as it circled lazily in the sky and then darted out of sight. He imagined that it spotted a rabbit or squirrel. He turned back to her. "What bothers me the most about all this is wondering what happened to Lester's thumb. If it was cut off in an accident, then where is it?"

Lydia shrugged and said she didn't know.

"This just doesn't make sense. If it was simply an accident, why didn't Jack bring Lester's thumb with him so it could be reattached...?"

"He said it was lost," Lydia said.

"What?"

"Jack said the thumb was lost," she repeated weakly.

"That doesn't make any sense."

"That's what he said."

Wolcott frowned, his lips straightening out into a hard line. He pushed himself out of his chair and told her he'd have Lester's doctor talk to her. He stopped at the door, took a deep breath, and informed her that Child Services was investigating the accident. "Until their investigation's complete Lester's going to have to be placed in a foster home. Bert, too. I'm sorry, Mrs. Durkin, but those are the rules."

"That's not right."

"There's nothing I can do about it," he said.

"It's still not right."

"Mrs. Durkin, what we have right now is a seventeen-year-old boy alone with his father having his thumb cut off and no reasonable explanation as to how it happened."

Lydia's took a tissue from her pocketbook. Her hand shook as she dabbed her eyes with it. "That woman who talked to me, the one wearing a turtleneck sweater in ninety degree weather, she's not with the hospital, is she?"

"Do you remember her name?"

Lydia found the woman's card. "Suzanne Phillips," she said. The card had a lot of acronyms and abbreviations on it and she had no idea what any of them stood for.

"Ms. Phillips is with Child Services," Wolcott said.

"How can you have a woman like that—someone without the sense to wear proper clothes during the summer—be allowed to make decisions like that about my family?"

"I don't know, Mrs. Durkin."

"It's not right."

Wolcott looked away from her and didn't answer.

"When's Bert and Lester going to be allowed to come home?"

Wolcott sighed and squeezed his eyes with his thumb and index finger. "I'll talk to Jack and Lester and see what they both have to say. If I can clear this up quickly enough, maybe tomorrow."

Lydia sniffed and gave Wolcott a hard look. "Well, make sure that you do that."

He hesitated for a moment with his hand on the doorknob, then walked back to her so he could give her a hand and escort her to the doctor who had performed Lester's surgery.

Time floated by Jack Durkin. One moment he'd be aware of weeding in one part of the field, next he'd be realizing that he was pulling out Aukowies fifty feet away from that spot. Somehow, even with his mind turning on and off like that, he survived it without any further injuries. He guessed he had gotten to the point where he could weed Aukowies in his sleep, which was a good thing since he was for the most part sleepwalking that afternoon. He was surprised when he was done with his last pass of the field and saw it was only six-thirty. Even with everything that had happened he had finished early.

Even with all the distractions . . .

Even with having to half-carry Lester the three miles back to their home . . .

He heaved the canvas sack over his shoulder and carried it to the stone pit. After dumping the Aukowie remains with all the others, he tossed a match onto the pile and watched it burst into flames. Once again they shot close to twenty feet upward, a bluish-reddish flame lighting the sky. It was an unnatural color for a fire, something that burning weeds shouldn't cause. It hit him then that he had planned to video-tape the flames. Up until that moment he had forgotten about Charlie Harper's video camcorder. After Lester lost his thumb he put the camcorder in the shed for safekeeping. He turned to retrieve it, but stopped after a couple of steps knowing the flames would be out by the time he got it. He turned back to the fire and watched it burn. It didn't matter. Lester had videotaped enough of that foot-high Aukowie in action before he dropped the camcorder . . .

The scene played back again in his mind, just as it had all afternoon. He had warned Lester what to expect, but the boy still thought it was all one big joke. When the foot-high Aukowie quit playing possum and whipped out at him, he was ready for it but his boy wasn't. He sidestepped the attack, then tried to pin the thing back with the spade.

Lester, who was standing a good ten feet away to his left, nearly dropped the camcorder then. Durkin glanced over his shoulder and saw the boy fumbling with it, his skin paling to a sick white. He yelled at him to just be careful and keep videotaping. He knew a one-foot high Aukowie didn't have anywhere near the strength of a fully matured one, but they could still surprise you. If he had been able to leverage his full body weight and strength properly he would've been able to pin that Aukowie to the ground, but he was reaching too much and didn't have his full weight behind him and the Aukowie was able to whip the spade out of his hands. It flew past Lester and almost hit him. Lester stumbled then. He dropped the camcorder also.

Durkin realized too late that Lester had reached down for the camcorder. It didn't click fast enough in his mind that it had fallen among two-inch high Aukowies. Before he could say anything he saw his son's thumb disappear. It was as if it had been chewed up by a buzz saw. He remembered the pink spray that came from it. He remembered Lester staring down at his hand, confused, trying to make sense out of what had happened. And then the screaming. Jesus, there was a lot of screaming. Even now in the dead stillness of the early evening he could hear traces of it.

He slapped Lester hard across the face then, trying to bring him out of his shock. Lester stopped screaming. He still whimpered and cried, but he stopped his screaming. Durkin needed to tie something around his son's hand. His own shirt was too dirty and damp with perspiration. He was afraid it would infect his son's wound, so he had Lester take his shirt off and he wrapped it tightly around Lester's damaged hand. After the shirt was tied as tightly as he could make it, Durkin picked up the camcorder and led Lester off the field. He had to keep telling his son to keep his hand held up. He didn't have to look down to know the rustling sounds were being made by baby Aukowies that had gotten a taste of human blood. Durkin left the camcorder in the shed and then brought Lester back home.

The flames died down. All that was left was a foul stench and a mound of smoldering ashes. He thought about Lester and wondered how his boy was doing. He wouldn't die from losing his thumb like that, not unless he bled to death or picked up a nasty infection. And Durkin couldn't help wishing that one of those two things would happen. He also couldn't help regretting not tying his own shirt around Lester's hand. While he felt ashamed for those thoughts, he no longer had any doubts about Lester. The boy was not cut out to be Caretaker. It was as simple as that. He couldn't risk the fate of the world in Lester's hands. Bert was going to have to be Caretaker. Durkin found himself alternately wishing Lester was okay and hoping his son would die.

He used a shovel that he had brought from the shed to bury the Aukowie ashes and mix in lime. When he was done he stored the shovel and canvas sack back in the shed and took the camcorder. He stood for a moment looking upwards at the barren sky overhead. Even in the early evening with the Aukowies weeded out, birds still avoided the area. All his years coming here he never once saw a bird fly over Lorne Field. Never saw any squirrels or chipmunks in the woods nearby either. He wondered whether it was like this in the winter when the Aukowies were deep underground and hibernating. He wondered if birds dared fly past the field then. He decided one day he'd have to come out and see for himself.

He started down the dirt path leading to the Caretaker's cabin. Thoughts about Lester bombarded him. He could see clearly the look on Lester's face as his son realized what had happened to his thumb, then how helpless Lester was when he had to be mostly carried those last two miles home. He tried to shake those images from his mind and instead focus on what he had to do. Bert needed to become the next Caretaker. Which meant that he was going to have to continue being Caretaker for another eight years. As hard as that sounded, he was going to have to accept that. It also meant he was going to have to take the necessary steps to make Bert his eldest son. Unless Lester died from losing too much blood. Or picked up a deadly infection . . .

All of Durkin's strength bled out of him as those thoughts crept into his mind. He grabbed onto a tree for support, his legs wobbly beneath him. He decided then that he would have to ignore the contract and transfer the Caretaker position to his second son. What was wrong with that? After losing his thumb, Lester was probably no longer even capable of doing the job. It was just common sense. Durkin felt better, less shaky, at least for the moment. Then all his recent transgressions came crashing down on him. First letting an Aukowie grow to one foot in height, then leaving the field before finishing his weeding for the day, and now this. Up until two days ago he had lived his life exactly to the letter of the contract, never wavering, never making any exceptions. As far as he knew, all Durkins before him had done the same. And now this.

The first Durkin to turn his back on the contract . . .

He was so damn cold. His tongue had turned fuzzy, like he had swallowed a wool sock.

The same one that his pa and grandpa and every Durkin before them held sacred. And now one intentional violation after the next . . .

His head reeled with that thought. The ground started to slip sideways on him. Then the sky went black and the earth rushed up to meet him, smacking him in the face. He didn't even feel it. He couldn't feel anything except being so damn cold. He tried to lift his head up through the blackness but couldn't.

Dear God, he thought, I'm going to die right now and nobody's going to be left to save the world. I do believe in you. Please, I want so much to believe in you.

He didn't die, though. He realized he had only fainted. After a minute or so the blackness started to fade. Slowly, he rolled onto his back. He lifted his hand in front of his eyes and could see its outline through a dim haze. He dropped his hand to his forehead, resting it there. His skin felt so damn clammy and wet. He shivered, realizing his shirt was drenched in cold sweat. After several more minutes he was able to push himself to a sitting position. He had dropped the camcorder when he fell and was now reaching out with his arms trying to locate it. He felt it, then gathered it up and pushed himself to his feet. He made a decision then. He wasn't going to violate the contract again. No more exceptions.

He steadied himself, waiting until he had some strength in his legs, then set off down the path again. He was surprised when he turned the next bend to see Sheriff Wolcott leaning against a tree.

"Jack," Wolcott said, nodding.

"What are you doing here?" Durkin asked, his voice coming out as a low croak. "You're not supposed to be out at Lorne Field. It's against the contract."

"I don't believe I'm at Lorne Field." Wolcott slapped his neck and studied the palm of his hand before wiping it against his pants leg. "I've been standing here waiting for you and getting bit up by mosquitoes. Damn things are the size of hummingbirds here. I don't know how the hell you stand it."

"What do you want?"

"Jesus, Jack, you know what I want. Your son had his thumb cut off. You need to tell me about it." Wolcott's eyes narrowed. "Jack, is something wrong? You look sick."

"Never mind how I'm feeling. You ain't my doctor."

Wolcott chuckled softly. "No, I'm not. But you don't look well at all. What happened out there today, Jack?"

"Didn't you talk to Lester yet?"

"Not yet. He's doped up on painkillers and his doctor asked me to wait 'til tomorrow."

Durkin felt lightheaded and almost lost his balance. He could see that Wolcott noticed it.

"So Lester's okay?" he asked.

"As okay as a seventeen-year-old boy can be after having his thumb chopped off."

"It wasn't chopped off."

Wolcott raised an eyebrow and waited for Durkin to explain further.

"Lydia knows what happened. She didn't tell you?"

"All she said was that there had been an accident."

"That's all she told you?"

"Jack, what happened?"

Durkin met Wolcott's eyes and told him that an Aukowie had gotten Lester's thumb.

"Come on, Jack—"

"I'm tellin' you what happened."

"You're kidding, right?"

"That's what happened."

"Damn it, Jack, I'm trying to give you every benefit of the doubt here." Grimacing suddenly, the sheriff slapped hard at his forearm, then his right ear. He looked back at Durkin and shook his head at him as if he were talking to a five-year-old child. "I need you to explain it to me, Jack."

"Don't you patronize me. Not after what I do for you and your family everyday."

"Yeah, I know, you save the world for us. Thanks, Jack, we appreciate it. But you have to tell me exactly how Lester lost his thumb. And telling me that an Aukowie got it isn't good enough."

"It ain't, huh? I wish I could take you down to that field so you could see for yourself."

"Is that a threat, Jack?"

"Nope, just something I wish I could do."

Wolcott straightened up, flinched and slapped the back of his neck. He searched the palm of his hand to see if he'd been quick enough. "Well, why don't we do that, Jack?" he offered.

"I can't. That would be violating my contract."

"You violated it earlier today, didn't you, Jack? When you brought Lester in from the field?"

Durkin's face reddened. "Yes, I did," he admitted.

"Of course you did," Wolcott said. "You had to. What else were you going to do? Leave your son out there to bleed to death?"

Durkin stared stone-faced at Wolcott. Wolcott waited for a response but didn't get any. He slapped at another mosquito, then sighed as he glanced at his watch.

"Look, Jack, it's getting late. I have a family to get home to. Why don't we take a walk back to the field and you can explain to me what happened."

Durkin didn't say anything, just continued to stare hard at the sheriff. Wolcott smiled pleasantly. "Come on, Jack," he said, "you violated your contract once today, what's one more time?"

"I ain't doing it. Not never again."

Wolcott started to sigh, then hopped to one side, ducking his head and brushing furiously at his ear. "Goddamn these mosquitoes!' he swore. He glared angrily at Durkin, his temper slipping away. "I want to hear right now what happened to Lester's thumb," he demanded, all signs of folksy pleasantness gone from his manner.

"Not much to tell. Lester dropped this camcorder. When he reached down to pick it up one of the Aukowies chewed his thumb off. It all happened too fast for me to do anything about it."

"You're telling me a weed bit off his thumb?"

"They ain't weeds."

Wolcott put a hand to his eyes and rubbed them with his thumb and index finger. He did for a while. When he took his hand away his eyes were rimmed with red. "Jack," he said, "you realize how nuts this sounds?"

"That's what happened. Ask Lester if you don't believe me."

"Jack, Jack, Jack," Wolcott repeated softly. "You're making this so damn hard on yourself. You want me to arrest you right now?"

"What for?"

"What for? How about maiming your son?"

"I didn't touch Lester. Ask him yourself."

"Sure. You didn't touch him. A weed bit off his thumb." Wolcott rubbed his eyes again, then pushed his hand through his hair. His hair was damp enough with sweat that it spiked up. "What was Lester doing with the camcorder?" he asked.

"He was helping me videotape those Aukowies in action."

"Yeah? You didn't by any chance videotape that weed biting off your son's thumb?"

"I don't know. Maybe. He was videotaping me trying to dig up one of the Aukowies when the damn thing whipped the spade out of my hands. That was when Lester stumbled and dropped the camcorder. Maybe it landed so it was pointing in the right direction to videotape what happened to Lester."

"So now you're telling me that a weed grabbed a spade out of your hands?"

"No, I said an Aukowie, not a weed."

"My mistake. An Aukowie. And let me guess, it threw the spade at your son."

"Yep."

Wolcott showed a tired smile. "And it hit Lester in the thumb, right? Chopped it right off?"

Durkin shook his head, scowling. "Nope, that's not what I said. The spade missed Lester. He had his thumb chewed off when he put it too close to an Aukowie. I kept warning him all afternoon not to do that."

Wolcott looked at Durkin and tried to make up his mind whether or not to keep humoring him. "Why don't you show me what you videotaped," he said finally.

Durkin pulled the view screen out from the camcorder and tried to play back the video. His scowl deepened as he stared at it. "I can't remember how to use this damn thing," he muttered.

"Give it to me."

Durkin handed Wolcott the camcorder. The sheriff tried to turn it on and frowned at it also. "I think it's broken," he said.

"Lester did drop it," Durkin said. He remembered with some shame dropping it also when he fainted. He remembered the ground around where he fell had been hard and that there were rocks there too, but he didn't mention any of that.

Wolcott examined the camcorder more carefully. "There's no tape inside."

"What?"

"There's no tape inside. See for yourself."

Wolcott pointed a finger at the empty slot where a tape should've been. Durkin squinted at it, shaking his head.

"That don't make any sense," he said. "There should be a tape there."

"Jack," Wolcott said, his expression turning grim, "why don't you quit wasting both our time and tell me what really happened at Lorne Field today."

"I'm telling you, there should be a tape in there. I don't understand why there ain't. There was one in it last night."

"It's empty now. Why is that?"

"I don't know."

"I'll tell you why. Because you took it out and got rid of it. I wouldn't be surprised if you buried it."

"Why would I do that?"

Wolcott looked at Durkin with a mix of exasperation and pity. He swallowed back what he wanted to say, which was that he did it because he was nuts. Instead he kept his voice as calm as he could and said, "Because somehow you've convinced yourself you could make a videotape proving that those weeds are monsters. But when the videotape showed they're nothing but weeds, you had to try something else. Is that why you cut off Lester's thumb? So you could claim they bit it off and prove they're monsters that way?

Come on, Jack, just admit this and let's make this easy for everyone. Especially your family."

"One of the Aukowies chewed off Lester's thumb," Durkin argued stubbornly.

"That's the story you're going to stick with?"

"It's the truth."

"I should arrest you right now," Wolcott said. "But if I did I'd have to drag you over a mile in handcuffs. No, with this I'm going to make sure to dot my *i*'s and cross my *t*'s. I'll wait until I talk to Lester. Besides, I know where to find you. You'll be back at Lorne Field tomorrow saving the world, won't you, Jack?"

"Make fun of me all you want."

"I'm simply asking you a question, Jack, that's all."

Durkin's eyes darkened. "Talk to Lester," he said. "He'll tell you what happened."

"I'm sure he will. I'll be seeing you, Jack."

Sheriff Wolcott handed the camcorder back to Durkin and nodded as he headed down an intersecting path leading to Hillside Drive where he had parked his car. Durkin stared dumbly at the camcorder in his large thick hands, wondering what had happened to the tape that had been inside it.

Chapter 6

Sheriff Wolcott waited five minutes and then backtracked to the path to Lorne Field. He knew if Durkin saw him heading to the field he'd go ballistic, and Wolcott had had just about enough of that man's craziness for one night.

If it had been anyone other than Durkin cutting off his son's thumb, he would've brought the person immediately to court to ask for a seventy-two-hour competency evaluation at the state mental hospital, but with Durkin involved it was more than simply worrying about whether all his *i*'s were dotted and his *t*'s crossed—he had to make sure his case against him was both thorough and air-tight. There were still some nuts around town who believed this bullshit story of monsters growing out of a field, not many, but enough that Wolcott had to make sure his case left no doubt about Durkin's actions. Before he could arrest Durkin he needed a statement from Lester and he needed to investigate the crime scene.

The sun was starting to set and in the early evening dusk he saw a brown bat flying erratically above him. The damn thing flew close enough a couple of times that he had to duck. He watched it cautiously for a minute, hoping it was busy eating its body weight in mosquitoes. After the bat flew out of sight, Wolcott headed down the path to Lorne Field.

After three-quarters of a mile, the path disappointingly narrowed to where it would be impossible to drive an off-road vehicle. It meant after he talked to Lester the following morning he'd have to park over a mile and a half from the field, hike that distance with a couple of deputies, handcuff Durkin and drag him back to the vehicle. Either that or let Durkin get one last day of weeding in before arresting him, which meant he'd have to miss dinner with his family two nights in a row. Thinking about that made him wish he could just arrest the crazy old coot and get it over with.

When he got within a half mile of the field he started jogging, more to outrun the mosquitoes than for any other reason, and was surprised at what he saw when he reached it. The field was large—maybe two football fields in width, one and a half in length, and it was completely barren. Absolutely nothing growing in it. No grass, no weeds, nothing. It was still light enough to see, but he turned his flashlight on and waved it over the field. If it weren't for the little holes and loose dirt everywhere, he'd have a hard time believing anything ever grew in it. As he thought about the effort required to walk up and down that field and pull out every little weed and blade of grass, he couldn't help but begrudgingly respect Durkin. The guy might be as crazy as a loon but he was sure as hell dedicated. Wolcott crouched on his heels so he could touch the ground. He picked up some dirt, rolled it between his thumb and fingers, then sniffed and tasted it. Nothing but ordinary dirt, just like any other field. He felt stupid and couldn't help self-consciously looking around to make sure no one was in eyeshot.

He walked over to a small dilapidated wooden structure that served as a shed. Inside were gardening tools, a wheelbarrow, shovel, spade and a canvas sack. He flashed the light on the edges of the tools. If there had been blood on any of them it had been wiped clean. He picked up the canvas sack and started to look inside but had to turn away. The stench was unbelievable. Like sulfur and ammonia and decay all mixed together. Keeping his head craned as far away as possible, he opened it and flashed his light inside and saw the sack was empty.

He left the shed and walked over to a stone pit about fifty yards to the left. Near the pit a large mound of lime had been dumped into a pile, probably a good hundred or so wheelbarrow loads worth. He wondered how Durkin brought all that lime to the field, but then he saw a pile of dirt that could easily have been a freshly dug grave and his thoughts gravitated elsewhere. He went back to the shed, retrieved the shovel and dug up the loose dirt. The original hole went no more than two feet deep, and after a while he realized that the only thing buried in it were ashes mixed with lime. He walked over to the stone pit and quickly turned away. The stench there was far worse than what had lingered in the canvas sack. He took a deep breath and held it before going back to the stone pit. Crouching again so he sat on his heels, he flashed a light inside the pit, then wiped his finger along it. More ash. Whatever weeds Durkin burned, he burned inside the pit. He could've just as easily burned the thumb there also or, for that matter, buried it anywhere within the field or along the woods. Wolcott thought about bringing dogs to the field, but decided it would be a waste of time. Anyway, if Lester told him what he was expecting, he wouldn't need the severed thumb to arrest Durkin.

He got out of his crouch and moved away from the stone pit before letting go of his breath and risking breathing in again. Traces of that stench still lingered and had somehow gotten into the back of his throat, making him feel like he could taste it. Tearing the wrapper off a pack of gum, he stuck two sticks in his mouth and chewed them, anything to get rid of that taste. Later he'd gargle a case of mouthwash if he had to. After a minute or so all he could taste and smell was the peppermint flavor of the gum. Relieved, he took a deep breath and, for the hell of it, walked out into the middle of the field. Standing there, he could've been standing in the middle of any plowed farm plot. Nothing special about it. Just that all the weeds and grass had been pulled out.

The noises running through his head slowly quieted down.

He realized how still it seemed. How unnaturally quiet it was for a country evening. No chirping, no buzzing, no noises of any kind.

And no mosquitoes.

When Jack Durkin arrived back at the cabin Lydia told him that Lester was being kept overnight at the hospital and that Child Services had come over earlier and taken Bert away.

"When the hospital releases Lester, he ain't going to be allowed to come home either. Not until they decide you had nothin' to do with Lester's accident."

Durkin didn't bother looking at her. He took one of the imported beers Charlie Harper had brought over and sat alone at the kitchen table. Later, when Lydia was at the stove, he told her in a tired monotone that Lester would tell them what happened and the boys would come home then.

Lydia had warmed up leftover pot roast for dinner and they ate quietly with neither of them looking at each other. Halfway through dinner Lydia asked him to just tell the truth about what happened to Lester.

"I know it must've been an accident," she said. "You were probably trying to show Lester how to dig up one of those weeds and something slipped. If you just tell people the truth everything will be able to go back as it was."

Durkin dropped his fork and knife onto his plate and looked up to meet Lydia's eyes. As he stared at her his own eyes became liquid. He sat motionless for no more than half a minute, but to Lydia it could've just as easily have been an hour, at least that's how long it seemed. He broke the silence by pounding on the table with his fist hard enough that the impact knocked a glass off the table and Lydia almost leapt out of her skin. The glass shattered into dozens of tiny shards with pieces scattering across the antique pine floor.

"If you think I'm going to clean that up, you're crazy," Lydia said.

Durkin's thick eyelids lowered an eighth of an inch as he stared at her. "You took the videotape out of that camcorder," he said.

"What? I don't know what you're talking about—"

"Don't lie to me. You think I'm stupid? After you kept telling me to wait on videotaping the Aukowies."

"I didn't do anything," she insisted stubbornly.

He pounded the table again. This time it had no effect on her.

"Goddamn it! I could've proven to the town that Aukowies are real. The videotape would've shown what they really are. Damn it, Lydia, why'd you have to do it?"

She had shifted her glance away from him. As she met his liquid eyes again, her own were as dry as sand.

"Why? Because I spoke with a lawyer yesterday who has a way for us to make a lot of money. More than you could imagine. But not if you start videotaping those weeds so you can prove to everyone they're nothin' but weeds. I'm not going to let you ruin this for us."

"Goddamn you—"

"You shut up! I have one son in the hospital and another taken out of my home, so you have no right to curse me or blame me for nothin'. You understand me?"

Durkin didn't say anything. A hot intensity burned on Lydia's small wrinkled face. Her hands clenched into tiny fists and her knuckles showed bone-white.

"If I thought for one second that you hurt Lester intentionally, I'd already be out the door, but not before putting a nice heaping spoonful of arsenic in that pot roast. Tomorrow morning you're going to admit to people what really happened. You're going to say that it was an accident and not a weed that bit off Lester's thumb."

Durkin didn't say anything. He just sat breathing hard, the moistness in his eyes quickly drying up.

"And why couldn't you bring Lester's thumb back with you?" Lydia demanded, thin veins streaking her neck and a large bluish one standing out in the middle of her forehead. "The doctors could've reattached it! Why couldn't you bring it back?"

"There was no thumb left."

"Shut up. Don't you try that nonsense with me!"

"But there wasn't," Durkin said. "Once the Aukowie was done with it there was no thumb."

"Shut up!" She hit the table herself with an open palm—not nearly as hard as her husband had, but hard enough to make a sharp crack. She grabbed her hand and held it as if it were broken. Tears welled up in her small eyes and started to leak down her cheeks. "Just shut up and quit talking this nonsense," she cried softly.

"Let me get some ice for that."

"I don't need any ice from you."

Durkin pushed himself away from the table, hobbled over to the cabinets making sure to avoid the broken glass littering the floor, then found a plastic bag and filled it with ice from the freezer. He brought the bag over to his wife and placed it gently against the hand she was holding.

"Do you think you broke it?" he asked.

"No, nothin's broke."

"Maybe I should take you to the hospital and have them check it?"

"Just sit down and finish your dinner."

Durkin opened his mouth to argue, but instead sat back down. He halfheartedly continued eating. Lydia watched him for a while, then told him the lawyer was going to be stopping by soon to explain how they were going to turn their lives around. "You're going to agree to whatever he says or so help me," she said, her voice not much more than a snake's hiss.

"I ain't violating the contract."

"You won't have to."

He nodded dully and went back to his food. He peeked at her a couple of times to try to figure how badly her hand was hurt and how he was going to get someone as stubborn as her to the hospital.

A few minutes before nine someone knocked on the front door. Lydia dumped the bag of half-melted ice into the kitchen sink then, before leaving to answer the door, warned her husband what she'd do to him if he ruined this for them. When she came back into the kitchen, she brought Paul Minter with her. He took a step towards Jack Durkin and then skipped to one side to avoid a piece of glass.

"You realize you have broken glass on your floor?" he asked Lydia.

"He'll clean it up," Lydia said, turning an angry glare towards her husband.

"The hell I will," Durkin muttered.

Minter looked at both of them. "If this is a bad time . . ." he started.

"As good a time as any." Lydia took her seat as stiffly as a corpse.

Minter gave them both curious looks again then, avoiding the broken glass, he made his way over to Durkin and introduced himself. Durkin grudgingly took his hand and muttered his own name in response. Minter carefully made his way over to Lester's seat at the table.

"Mr. Durkin, it's a pleasure meeting you." Minter looked around the room smiling artificially. "Has your wife mentioned to you any of what we're planning?"

"Nope. Not a word."

Durkin snuck a quick look at his wife and couldn't help worrying about how awkwardly she held her injured hand. He also didn't think this kid sitting at the table with them seemed like much of a lawyer. He sure wasn't dressed like one, wearing a polo shirt and short pants, and without anywhere near the imposing presence of someone like Hank Thompson. Durkin wiped his hand off with his napkin and watched as Paul Minter showed off a large toothy grin.

"Well, it's really pretty simple." Minter adjusted himself in his seat and took one more gaze around the room. "What we'd like to do is develop a theme park around what you do."

"I don't follow you."

"We're going to put this town on the map. Instead of

people spending money to go to Salem, Massachusetts, for witch trials, we'll get them to spend money here watching monsters being pulled out of the earth. Imagine this house being turned into a museum and gift shop—"

"Wait a minute. Where are we supposed to live?"

"We'll build you a new house," Minter said with a wide smile. "With the numbers the investors are tossing around, we should be able to build you something nice. Central air, central vacuum, gourmet kitchen, home theatre, pool and Jacuzzi in back. How does all that sound?"

"Sounds okay," Jack Durkin admitted. "But it's going to have to be close by so I can get back and forth to that field."

"That's not going to be a problem. There's quite a bit of land deeded with this cabin for us to build on. Getting back to what I was saying, along with this house being turned into a museum and gift shop, we'll offer tours to Lorne Field so people can watch you at work, and—"

"I ain't allowing nothin' that goes against the contract. No one's allowed at Lorne Field but me."

Minter forced his smile wider. "Contracts can be amended—"

"Nope. Not this one. It ain't being changed. Not a word of it. Everything in it is written for a reason. You start messing around with it and we're all lost."

'Please, Mr. Durkin, you need to be reasonable—"

"I'm not allowing a single word of that contract to be changed. Not a single damn word."

"Is there anything in the contract against turning this home into a museum or gift shop?" Lydia asked.

Durkin thought about it and shook his head.

"How about against you setting up cameras down there so people can watch you work?"

Again Durkin ended up admitting that there wasn't.

Lydia turned to Minter. "How about all that then?" she asked. "Would that be good enough?"

Minter pursed his lips as he considered it. "I think that would work," he said. "We could clear out some land behind this cabin and recreate Lorne Field. It might even be better that way. It would both add to the mystique of the actual field and give us more control. And people wouldn't have to traipse miles through woods to get there. I'd still like to have a supply of weeds that we could laminate and sell as souvenirs."

Durkin's jaw dropped as he digested what the lawyer was suggesting. "W-what do you want to do?" he stammered out, not sure he believed that he had heard right.

"We could make a small fortune selling those weeds."

"Over my dead body."

"Okay, okay." Minter held out a hand to stop him. "I just thought I'd ask. The marketing potential could be huge for something like that. But it's not a deal breaker."

"So we're all set?" Lydia asked.

"Well, we'll see. The investors I talked to so far are excited, and I think I have the support of the town council. So as long your husband doesn't have any further objections . . . ?"

Durkin glanced at his wife and saw that her eyes were fixed on him. He also saw her still gingerly holding her injured hand. "As long as it don't violate my contract, you and my wife can do whatever you want." He cleared his throat. "What would be in the museum?" he asked somewhat sheepishly.

"Quite a lot, actually. A complete history of Lorne Field, the legend of its monsters and, of course, paintings and sculptures of them, along with portraits and a short biography of each of your ancestors who've been Caretaker and, as your wife brilliantly suggested, video monitors so people can watch you at work. You are going to continue weeding the field, right?"

"Why wouldn't I?"

"I'm just asking."

"I'll be weeding the field until my eldest son takes over. As required by my contract."

"That's good," Minter said. He was still smiling broadly, but it was beginning to lose some of its luster. "It will give the whole thing an air of realism. Kind of a Colonial Williamsburg-type vibe. And of course the centerpiece for the museum will be the Caretaker's Contract and Book of Aukowies under a glass display."

"How do you know about my book?"

"Your wife told me about it."

Jack Durkin shifted a suspicious glance towards Lydia, then grunted as he pushed himself away from the table.

"Let me get it for you so you can see it for yourself," he said. "And the contract, too."

Durkin left the kitchen, careful to avoid the broken shards of glass littering the floor, and hobbled down the narrow basement steps. He stopped when he found the two loose stones. They weren't pushed back as deep as they should've been. He knew he didn't make that kind of mistake and guessed that either Lydia or Bert had found his hiding place, knowing that Lester wouldn't have had the initiative. It was too bad. The hiding place had been used by the eldest Durkin ever since the cabin was built, but he decided it no longer mattered. The whole damn place was going to be made into a freak show soon anyway. But at least it would get Lydia off his back. And with video cameras at Lorne

Field, people would see what the Aukowies really were. They'd all learn soon enough that this was no joke.

He took the contract and the Book of Aukowies out of their hiding place and brought them back upstairs. He dropped them in front of the lawyer and told him to feel free to take a look at them. With the cursory glances the lawyer gave them, Durkin knew he had seen them before, which meant Lydia had found his hiding place. He felt better knowing that. He would've hated to think Bert would've been so sloppy as to leave the stones pushed only three-quarters of the way in.

"Why don't you read the contract more carefully," he suggested. "I got some questions for you about it."

Minter showed him a puzzled smile. "What questions?"

"Let me show you." Jack Durkin took the contract in his hands and ran a thick index finger down the vellum paper until he found the clause he was looking for. "About what it says here—" Durkin stopped for a moment to squint hard at the paper, then he read out loud: "No person may interfere with the Caretaker from carrying out his sacred duties."

"Yes?"

"Can that be legally enforced?"

"What do you mean?"

"Jack," Lydia interrupt, "don't bother Mr. Minter with this."

He ignored her and went on. "I think Sheriff Wolcott is planning to arrest me."

Minter blinked stupidly, but kept smiling. "Why is he planning to do that?"

"He's claiming I cut off my son's thumb."

Minter's face fell. "What?"

"There was an accident today," Lydia said. "Jack took

our oldest boy, Lester, to that field to teach him how to weed and there was an accident."

"Is that true, Mr. Durkin? Your son had an accident today?"

"Yep."

"How—I mean, what happened?"

"My son lost his thumb."

"Yes I know, that part I heard. How did it happen?"

"An Aukowie chewed it off."

"What do you mean?"

Durkin shrugged. "Just what I said. Lester put his thumb too close to an Aukowie and it chewed it off."

Minter looked from Durkin to Lydia hoping to see that this was some kind of joke. All he saw in Lydia's face was resignation, and in Durkin's a stubborn earnestness.

"You're serious?" he said.

"That's what happened."

"And this is what you told Sheriff Wolcott?"

"It's what happened."

Minter looked back and forth at them. His wide apple-cheeked face pinched in concern. "I've put in a lot of time already talking to these investors and the town council. Not only that, but my reputation . . ." he started, his words choking off.

"I'm just telling you what happened."

"Has your son told his side of the story to the authorities yet?"

"No. Sheriff Wolcott told me that the doctors want him to wait until tomorrow to talk to Lester."

"Have you talked to your son yet?"

"Not yet. He was crying too much after it happened and I was just trying to get him home before he bled to death."

Durkin wiped a hand across his jaw, then tugged at his grizzled chin as he thought about Lester and what had happened. "I'm planning to go to the hospital after dinner to see how he's doing."

"They won't let you see him," Lydia said.

Durkin stared at her as if she were crazy.

"Neither of us are allowed to see him," Lydia repeated dismally. "Not until Child Services finishes their investigation."

"That's not right—"

"What will your son say about what happened to him?" Minter asked, cutting him off.

Durkin looked dumbly at the lawyer as if he had forgotten who he was. "He'll say the same as me. That one of the Aukowies chewed off his thumb."

Minter lowered his head into his left hand and squeezed his eyes as if he had a migraine.

"To answer your earlier question," he said, "that clause would not withstand scrutiny by the courts. It's not a get-out-of-jail-free card. You can be arrested and sent to prison."

He stopped squeezing his eyes and stood up abruptly. He nodded to Lydia and Durkin. "I'll be speaking to you soon," he said to Lydia, then to Durkin, "If you're arrested call me immediately. From this point on if Sheriff Wolcott or any other official asks you what happened to your son tell them it was an accident. Or better yet, don't say a word and have them talk to me instead. And most importantly, do not make any videotapes of those weeds. Keep a low profile, do not do anything to call further attention to yourself, and do not, I repeat, do not make any videotapes of those weeds. Do we understand each other?"

Durkin stood glumly with his arms crossed and his stare cast down to the floor.

"Mr. Durkin, am I getting through to you?"

Durkin nodded slowly.

"Good." He sighed heavily. "Right now I'd better go and see if I can have a talk with your son. Mrs. Durkin, what hospital is he at?"

"First Baptist."

Minter nodded, repeated that he'd be speaking to them soon and headed towards the front door. Glass crunched under his tennis sneakers. He didn't seem to notice. Lydia yelled out to him, asking whether this was going to change their plans.

Minter stopped and gave her a tired look. "I hope not," he said. "No, it shouldn't. If it was an accident like you say, then it shouldn't matter. It might make our investors skittish for a week or two, but that will hopefully be the extent of it."

He nodded once more to them and then hurried from the room. They heard the front door open and close only seconds later.

Lydia sat frozen, her small wrinkled face twenty years older than earlier that evening. At that moment Jack Durkin had a good idea how his wife would look on her deathbed. It also made him think of a magician's trick. Lower the curtain and raise it a second later to reveal that the middle-aged woman volunteer has been replaced by her elderly mother. She stared straight back at him without appearing to notice him. Slowly recognition seeped into her eyes.

"You're not going to ruin this for me," she said in a quiet, dispassionate voice. "Not just for me, but for Lester and for Bert. Do you understand that?"

"Look, I haven't done anything."

"I asked if you understand me?"

Durkin saw cold violent murder in her eyes and nodded accordingly.

"You are going to do exactly what that lawyer told you to do. And you're not going to say another word to anyone about a weed biting off Lester's thumb. If you do, so help me God."

She stood up awkwardly, tottering for a few seconds on her feet before getting her balance. Durkin felt sick inside seeing how she held her injured hand and how swollen it had gotten.

"You need to have a doctor look at that," he said.

"Only thing you should be worrying about now is how you're going to explain to Daniel Wolcott why you didn't have Lester's thumb with you when you brought him home."

He sat and watched her leave the kitchen, then listened to the sound of her heels clacking across the living room's hardwood floor and later on the stairs leading to the second floor. When the sounds faded, he found the broom and dustpan and swept up the broken glass. After that he washed and dried the dishes.

The more he thought about it the more that lawyer's plans sounded like pie-in-the-sky dreaming to him, but if Lydia wanted to believe it then he'd let her. He didn't see any harm coming from it, and if it gave her some hope, all the better. Eventually he'd get the town to increase his honorarium, and once that happened, Lydia would settle down. As far as Wolcott went, he pretty much expected the sheriff's reaction to what he told him. But what else was he going to say? Make something up? He'd pay anything, though, to see Wolcott's reaction when Lester told him his side of the story. Wolcott always treated him as a crank, as if what he did was one big joke, and he'd love to see the look on that smug bastard's face once it dawned on him that maybe the Aukowies were something other than weeds. The only problem was if Lester couldn't remember what happened. He had a nagging fear that that might happen. It seemed as if Lester went into shock almost immediately, and if he did and had somehow blocked out his memories of dropping the camcorder and having his thumb chewed off, then Wolcott would continue his snickering and treating him like the town loon. Worse, he'd probably arrest him and keep him from weeding Lorne Field. That thought had worried him most of the afternoon.

Durkin fished through Lydia's junk drawer where she kept coupons and recipes and other odds and ends. In the back of it he found a torn piece of paper that had been sitting in there for years. The ink was mostly faded, but Durkin could still make out the phone number written on it.

He picked up the phone and called the last number he had for his brother. It had been almost ten years since Joe called and left the number with Lydia, and almost twenty-five years since Durkin last spoke to his brother. He had no idea whether the number was still good, but he prayed that it was.

Joe answered after the fifth ring.

"What do you know," he said, "my big brother, Jack, calling. Never thought I'd hear from you again."

"How'd you know it was me?"

Joe laughed. "Caller ID. You should get it and join the twenty-first century."

"Joe, I need your help."

"What, no pleasantries? After what, twenty, twenty-five years—that's all I get from you, that you need help? You can't even pretend to ask how me or my family's doing? But then again you're a busy man saving the world each day."

"What are you trying to say? That you don't believe I save the world each day?"

"I don't know." There was a long pause, then, "Look, Jack, you drank the Kool-Aid, I only sniffed it. I just don't know."

"You think I'm crazy then," Durkin said angrily. "And pa and grandpa and every other Durkin before them. And you're the only sane one of us 'cause you got to go off to college."

"Jack, I'm not saying any of you are crazy, but this is something I've thought a lot about since leaving home. Maybe there's some other explanation. For example, maybe the weeds secrete a mild hallucinogenic that can be absorbed through the skin when you touch them—"

"I don't touch them. I wear gloves."

"Do you wear latex gloves underneath?"

"What? No."

"Then it could still be aborbed through the gloves and then into the skin. Or through the air. Or maybe the Aukowies are exactly what pa and grandpa always said they were. Anyway, don't get mad, I'm not saying any of this to upset you. It's been on my mind, that's all. So how much do you need?"

"I don't need money from you."

"Then what?"

"I might need you to take over for me."

"Jack—"

"I might not be able to do this much longer."

"Jack, I can't do that. I've got a wife and family. Three daughters and a son, not that you ever bothered to ask. I can't just pack up and move halfway across the country."

"They might throw me in jail tomorrow. Somebody's got to weed the Aukowies if I can't. It's only two months or so 'til first frost. That's all I'm asking."

"Why are you going to be thrown in jail?"

Durkin rubbed some wetness from his eyes. "It's not important," he said. "It ain't definite either. So you going to come if I need you to?"

"Jack, I can't."

"All I'm asking for is two months. Joe, I've been doing this over thirty years, and you know everything I gave up to do this. You can give me two months . . . Joe? Hello, Joe, are you still there?"

"Yeah, I'm still here. I'm sorry, Jack, I can't. Listen, if they're nothing but weeds then there's no point in me taking over for you, but if they're what pa and grandpa said they were, then it wouldn't make any difference whether I tried weeding them or not because they'd rip me to shreds the first day I was out there. Remember, Jack, pa spent a whole summer teaching you how to weed them. Besides, I'd be violating the contract."

Red flashed brightly in Durkin's brain and burned deeply. He stood trembling as he held the phone, only half-aware of telling his brother to go fuck himself and putting the receiver down. It was a long time before the red faded and he could breathe normally again. He moved back to the kitchen table and sat down. He buried his face in his hands and wept until there was nothing left inside. Until he felt completely empty. Then he wiped his face off with the dish towel and went upstairs to join Lydia in bed.

Chapter 7

The next morning Jack Durkin was out of bed two hours earlier than usual. Keeping as quiet as he could, he snuck down to the kitchen, poured himself a bowl of cereal, made a cup of instant coffee and was out the door before Lydia woke up, or at least before she had a chance to come downstairs and nag at him. He was two-thirds done with his second pass of weeding when Wolcott and two town police officers, Bob Smith and Mark Griestein, approached the field. The three men walked up to him, and Wolcott told him he was under arrest for cutting off his son's thumb.

"It's a long hike back to the cruiser, Jack. I'm hoping I don't have to put handcuffs on you. You'll come along peacefully, won't you?"

Durkin nodded. He looked from Wolcott to the other two men with him. Griestein's face was a blank screen, his eyes shielded by mirrored sunglasses. Bob Smith, on the other hand, looked deeply worried. Durkin had finished his freshman year of high school before dropping out. During that year he played third base for his school's varsity baseball team, while Bob Smith, a senior, played first. His coach thought Durkin had major league potential, and so did the scouts who came to watch him play. That was the reason he dropped out after one year; he didn't want to hear about all the potential he had when his future was already set. But during that season him and Bob had been good friends.

"Okay, Jack," Wolcott said, "you can leave the canvas sack where it is. Let's go."

The last thing Durkin wanted to do was give Wolcott any satisfaction, but he couldn't stop himself from saying how an Aukowie chewed off Lester's thumb and if his boy couldn't remember what had happened it was because of his being in shock.

"Is that so?" Wolcott said. "One of these weeds bit it off, huh? It's funny, to me they only look like weeds. Maybe godawful ugly ones, but still just weeds. How about you, Mark? These weeds look like they could bite off someone's thumb?"

Griestein shook his head.

"How about you, Bob?" Wolcott asked. "You think they could do something like that?"

"Dan, let's just do our job and get out of here."

"One minute. I just want to see how hungry these man-eating weeds really are." Wolcott walked over to a clump of two-inch Aukowies and lowered his hand towards them. Durkin closed his eyes. He didn't want to watch what was going to happen. After several seconds of squeezing his eyes shut tight, he was surprised when he didn't hear any screaming.

"Come on, Jack," Wolcott said, "take a look for yourself and tell me why my fingers aren't being bitten off."

Jack Durkin opened his eyes. Wolcott's fingers were right in the middle of the Aukowies. He could see their little faces as they smirked at him, and he understood.

They knew.

How?

Somehow they knew they could hurt him if they resisted their natural urges. That they could beat him this way. But he could see the strain building on them. He could see them weakening.

"Just keep your fingers where they are," Durkin said.

Wolcott stood up, not bothering to hide the disgust on his face. "Come on, Jack, let's get you to the station."

Griestein nudged Durkin, and he followed behind Wolcott while the two police officers stayed on either side of him.

"You don't know what you're doing," Durkin told Wolcott. "Without me weeding they're going to be four to five inches by nighttime."

"I'm doing my job, Jack. That's all I'm doing."

When they got onto the path leading back to the cabin, Durkin asked if they could stop by his house so he could tell Lydia what was happening.

"Sorry, Jack, I need to take you to the station. After you're processed, you can make a phone call."

Bob Smith glared at Wolcott, then over Wolcott's protestations, handed Durkin his cell phone. "Go ahead, Jack," he said, "give Lydia a call."

Durkin stared at the phone as if he were being asked to perform an emergency appendectomy. Trying to keep his voice low so Wolcott couldn't hear him, he admitted that he didn't know how to use it. Even if he did, he doubted whether he'd even be able to push the buttons on it with his fingers being as thick and swollen as they were. Bob Smith asked for his home number and dialed it for him. When Lydia picked up, Durkin told her he was being arrested and for her to bring his contract to Hank Thompson and tell him what was happening. "I know you know where it's hidden, so don't try arguing otherwise. And I don't want that other lawyer involved."

Durkin handed the cell phone back to Bob Smith and thanked him for his help. Bob Smith looked like he badly wanted to ask him a question, but he restrained himself.

❦

Even though Lydia had been expecting that very call from her husband all morning, it was still a shock after she got off the phone with him. She sat at the table and chain-smoked through half a pack of cigarettes before she felt like she could move. Then she brought the phone to the kitchen table and tried to make up her mind about what to do.

Her right hand, the one she had injured hitting the table, had swollen to twice its normal size and was a pur-plish-bluish color around the base of her palm. It hurt too much for her to hold the receiver in it, so she had to rest the receiver on the table while she dialed with her left hand and then picked it up also with her left hand. When she told the receptionist who she was, she was put on hold for five minutes before Paul Minter answered. His voice sounded odd as he told her it was over.

"What?"

"It's over, Mrs. Durkin."

"What do you mean it's over?"

He sighed. "Just what I said. The town council doesn't want anything to do with this anymore. I spoke with all of them and it's over."

Her head was spinning as she tried to get a handle on what he was telling her. Not that it surprised her. Not that it wasn't exactly what she was expecting. Ever since the lawyer told her they could make millions she knew Jack would ruin it for them.

"This doesn't make any sense," she said, although she

knew it made perfect sense, but she still couldn't help herself asking why it was happening.

He sighed again. "Because your son, Lester, is telling the authorities that your husband grabbed him, wrestled him to the ground and cut off his thumb. I understand that the police are going to be arresting him soon. It's probably better if you hire another lawyer to represent him."

He hung up then.

She sat clutching the phone for another few minutes before heading upstairs to the bedroom to pack her clothes away in a small tattered cloth suitcase that she had last used nineteen years earlier when Jack took her on a trip to Miami. When she was done she called her friend, Helen Vernon. After that, she smoked a couple of more cigarettes, carried her suitcase out to Jack's Chevy Nova and, with some effort, swung it into the trunk. She stood frozen for a long moment. When she looked back at the house, she daydreamed about lighting a match to it. In her mind's eye she could see it going up in flames. But she didn't light any matches. Instead, she got in the car and drove away.

Hank Thompson showed up at the police station while Jack Durkin was being fingerprinted. He was a tall, lean man in his early seventies with a thick bushy head of hair the color of cigar ash and an imposing air of authority about him. He waited until Durkin wiped the ink from his fingers, then offered his hand.

"I'm so sorry about your son's accident," he said with the utmost sincerity.

Durkin started to open his mouth to correct him, but

closed it and nodded instead. "Lydia call you?" he asked. "I'm surprised she ain't here yet."

Hank Thompson's thick cigar-ash-colored eyebrows came together as he frowned and shook his head. "No, I haven't heard from your lovely wife yet. Officer Bob Smith called me to let me know what happened, but I also heard through the grapevine."

"Hank, I need to get back to that field."

Hank Thompson was still holding Durkin's hand, and he placed his free hand on top of Durkin's and gave it a warm pat. An understanding and comforting smile formed over his lips. "I know you do, Jack," he said. "And I'm going to get you back there as soon as I possibly can." The attorney turned to Officer Mark Griestein who was processing Durkin and told him in a pleasant but firm voice that he'd like to have a few minutes alone with his client. Griestein scratched behind his ear, nodded, and led the way to a storage chamber that doubled as a conference room, although up to that point it had never been used that way.

"I'll be out here," he told them. "Take your time."

As soon as the door closed Hank turned to Jack and, with his voice trembling with indignation, said, "This is outrageous what they're doing to you."

"They violated my contract. They marched right onto Lorne Field and violated my contract."

"It's not right, Jack, not after everything you and your family has done for this town. I knew your dad well. He was a good man. This is just not right. But—" and he waved a long thin finger for emphasis, "it's going to be taken care of. I've already spoken to Judge Harris and he's heading to the courthouse as we speak. When he gets there, he's going to open a special session for your arraignment hearing. Those bastards were planning to keep you locked up in jail overnight so they could make a big show of the hearing tomorrow morning."

"I thought Judge Harris retired?"

Hank showed a sly, secretive smile. "Not entirely. He put off the paperwork so he could be called in as a consultant if needed. And Jack, that is very good news for us."

Hank's cell phone rang. He frowned as he held it at arm's length so he could read the caller ID information, then he spoke quickly in it before hanging up.

"Good news. Judge Harris is at the courthouse now," he told Durkin. "We'll get you over there in about fifteen minutes and then back to your field."

"I hope so," Durkin muttered in a low guttural voice. "Two-inch Aukowies are hard enough to weed. Once they get to four to five inches . . ."

"I understand, Jack. You don't have to say any more." Hank cleared his throat, his smile weakening a bit. "How are you going to explain to Judge Harris about what happened?"

"I'll tell him the truth."

"That it was an accident, right, Jack?" Hank placed a hand on Jack Durkin's shoulder and stooped down several inches so he could meet Durkin's eyes. "That's what you're going to tell him, right?"

Durkin nodded slowly as if he had had weights attached to the back of his head.

"That is the truth, isn't it, Jack? That it was an accident?"

"Yep. You could call it an accident."

"Good." Hank nodded slowly as he assessed Durkin. "Any idea what your son has told the police?"

"All I can think is he can't remember what happened. He seemed to go into shock pretty fast."

"That must be it," Hank agreed with more certainty. "Those bastards trying to make a case out of this." He turned away and rapped his knuckles hard against the door. When Griestein opened it, Hank told him his client was expected in court for his arraignment hearing.

"I thought it was tomorrow."

"No, sir. You can call over there if you'd like."

Griestein made a face over the prospect of having to do that. He led Durkin and his attorney to the front desk while he called the courthouse. He seemed surprised to find that Hank had his facts straight. "I didn't think it was going to be until tomorrow," he muttered to himself as he hung up the phone.

Over at the courthouse they had to wait twenty minutes until a flustered county attorney, Jill Bracken, arrived with Dan Wolcott at her side. Bracken was in her early thirties, slender yet athletic, and would've been attractive except for all the sharp edges on her. She wore a steel-gray suit that matched the color of her eyes and had her shoulder-length blond hair rolled up into a tight bun. She started to sputter immediately to Judge Harris that this was highly unusual to schedule an arraignment hearing so quickly. "I haven't had a chance to prepare yet," she said as she fumbled with a pile of notes.

Judge Harris held out a hand to stop her, an impatient frown showing on his round face. "Counsellor, if you're going to have the defendant arrested, then you should be prepared to read the charges filed against him. Tell me that you are prepared."

Red blotches showed along Jill Bracken's cheeks. "Yes, your honor. The defendant is charged with aggravated assault."

"And how is that?"

"He used a knife to cut off his son's thumb."

Judge Harris turned to Hank. "And your client's side of the story?"

"It was an accident, your honor."

"Is that what happened, Mr. Durkin?"

Jack Durkin nodded.

Judge Harris picked up a trial calendar and frowned at it. "Unless there are any objections the trial date will be set for November second. Mr. Thompson, you will guarantee that your client will appear in this court on that date?"

"Yes, your honor."

"At this time I see no reason to impose bail. The defendant is free to go until then."

Jill Bracken nodded as she arranged the stack of papers in front of her, but Wolcott whispered intently to her, then spoke out. "Judge, I was the arresting officer. I believe this man is a danger to the community and he should be committed for a seventy-two-hour psych evaluation."

Judge Harris stared hard at Wolcott, annoyance deepening his frown. He started to tap his fingers along his bench. "Sheriff Wolcott, I don't believe I asked for your opinion—"

"Judge, I have a sworn statement from his son, Lester, that Mr. Durkin tackled him to the ground and then held him down as he cut off his thumb."

Judge Harris blanched at hearing that. He shot Hank Thompson a questioning look before turning back to Wolcott.

"Why would Mr. Durkin do that?"

Wolcott laughed sourly. "Somehow he got it in his head that he could convince the town a weed bit his son's thumb off."

"Are there other injuries consistent with the type of struggle that you described?"

"The boy's thumb was cut off!"

"I understand that, but were there other injuries, such as scrapes or cuts, that would be consistent with the boy being tackled to the ground?"

Wolcott consulted with Jill Bracken as the two of them searched through her notes.

"I'm not prepared to answer that at this time," he said.

"Well, you should be. Any other reasons to call Mr. Durkin's mental state into question?"

"I'd have to think so. He believes the weeds at Lorne Field are some kind of monsters."

"That's a lie," Jack Durkin said. "Don't go putting words in my mouth."

"You haven't been telling me those are monsters out there?"

"As far as I'm concerned I'm only honoring a contract with this town and pulling out weeds every day as my contract requires. Nothing more."

Judge Harris smiled at that. Hank gave Durkin a wink. Jill Bracken consulted furiously with her notes. Wolcott stared flabbergasted at Durkin.

"Judge, this man told me just the other day that a weed bit off his son's thumb. Also some boys snuck down to Lorne Field and pelted him with tomatoes. He wanted me to find them so they could be publicly executed!"

Judge Harris tapped his fingers harder along the bench. "Is that true?"

Durkin shook his head. "No, sir. I showed him where in my contract it calls for that, but all I wanted him to do was find those boys so they could help out with my weeding as punishment."

"Sounds reasonable," Judge Harris agreed.

"Judge, he's lying! That's not how our conversation went!" Wolcott, his face flushed, stared open-mouthed at Durkin before turning back to face Judge Harris. "I learned this morning that Lester was one of the boys who pelted Mr. Durkin with tomatoes. I can't help thinking that he found out and cut off Lester's thumb as some sort of retaliation."

"How do you know Lester was one of them?" Durkin asked, his voice a low rumble.

"Bert told me. Lester confirmed it," Wolcott said without looking at him.

Durkin's head dropped a few inches, his eyes mostly lifeless. For that split second he could've been a man heading to the gallows. Hank Thompson clapped him on the shoulder for support and sent a glare towards Wolcott.

"Mr. Durkin," Judge Harris asked, his voice contrite, "did you know your son was involved?"

Durkin shook his head. "I had no idea."

Wolcott made a noise as if something had caught in his sinuses. Judge Harris's frown turned even more dour as he faced him. "Sheriff Wolcott, your accusations here have been scattered, at best. First Mr. Durkin committed this crime as part of a ruse, then as an act of revenge. Mr. Durkin has carried himself with the utmost decorum, while you, sir, have been the only one here who seems to be having difficulty controlling his emotions or thought processes. You're one outburst away from seeing me do as you're requesting and ordering a psychiatric evaluation, but not for Mr. Durkin. Do I make myself clear?"

Wolcott nodded, a darkness muddling his face.

Judge Harris watched him for a moment, then told Durkin that he was free to go but to be prepared to be back in court November second for his trial. "Although lacking additional physical evidence, it seems hard to consider your son's statement credible," he added under his breath.

Hank Thompson led Durkin towards the door, but before they reached it Wolcott caught up to them.

"Hank, you know I'm only trying to do my job here."

"It sounded personal to me."

"Not at all. I honestly believe Mr. Durkin needs help, and I hope for his sake that you see that he gets it."

"I'll take your concerns under advisement." Hank turned his back on Wolcott and ushered Durkin out of the building.

"Let's get you back where you belong," he said.

Officer Bob Smith was waiting on the sidewalk, his hands stuck in his pockets and a forlorn look spread across his face. He walked slowly to Durkin and held out his hand.

"I'm sorry about what happened."

Durkin nodded and took his hand.

"I hated what I had to do today. More than anyone else in this town I know everything you gave up."

Durkin again felt like Smith wanted to ask him something, but the other man turned and walked away.

Hank Thompson offered to drive Durkin down Hillside Drive so he could pick up the path from there to Lorne Field. "It should be a shorter walk to Lorne Field that way than taking you home."

Durkin agreed and got into Hank's older model Cadillac sedan.

"If you'd like we could get you a bite to eat first," Hank suggested.

"Thanks for the offer, but I'd better just get back there. It's late, and those Aukowies are growing every second. It's going to be tough enough as it is."

Like Officer Bob Smith, Hank seemed to have a question he wanted to ask. Durkin could see it in his eyes. After they got through the first traffic light on Main Street, the attorney finally broached the subject of Lester's statement. "Any idea why your son might have said that?"

Durkin shook his head. "All I can think is he was in shock and didn't know what happened. Maybe Dan Wolcott put the idea in his head."

"That must be it," Hank agreed after mulling it over. "I'd have to think your boy was so traumatized by the accident that he'd be vulnerable to suggestive or poorly phrased questions by our good sheriff. Don't worry, Jack, I'll find a psychiatrist who will testify to that. This case won't be a problem, especially as long as we've got Judge Harris hearing it."

Durkin stared mutely out the window and watched as they left Main Street behind. Once they got to the intersection leading to Hillside Drive, he told Hank Thompson that an Aukowie did bite off his son's thumb.

"I'm not crazy," he said. "I saw it with my own two eyes."

Hank Thompson smiled thinly. "I'd say something about believing you, except admitting to something like that is not a politically smart thing to do these days. If my kids heard me, they'd have me declared mentally incompetent so fast it would leave your head spinning. Jack, let's just say I sleep better at night knowing you're at that field everyday.

And I'd be willing to bet that Judge Harris sleeps better, too."

Durkin nodded as he accepted that. "Anything you can do about Sheriff Wolcott and those others violating my contract?"

"At this point it's probably best not to make an issue about it, especially with the town council we have now. Best to just lay low for the time being."

"Why? What do you think the town council would do?"

Hank made a face like he had swallowed sour milk. "Let's not worry ourselves about that. Let's concentrate first on getting you cleared of these charges."

Hank slowed down to look for the dead oak tree stump that marked the head of the path Durkin needed to take. After he spotted it, he pulled over and offered Durkin his hand.

"Jack, the words don't exist to express how outraged I am over what happened today." He paused for a moment, his long brow furrowing with concern. "You'll be okay out there?"

"I'd better be." Durkin took Hank's hand, nodded grimly and set off towards Lorne Field.

It had been twelve-thirty when Wolcott and the two police officers trespassed onto Lorne Field and dragged him away from his duties. It was now ten minutes to four. Over three hours had passed, which meant the Aukowies he hadn't gotten to during his second pass of weeding would now be over five inches tall. The thought of that weakened him. But with all the indignities he had been forced to suffer that day, it did help to know that there were people like Bob Smith and Hank Thompson and Judge Harris who believed in what he did even if they wouldn't actually come out and say so. That both helped him and infuriated him. The most important job in the world and this is what it has come down to, hoping that a few people would still understand the importance of what he did.

Even his own son . . .

He was puzzled by why Lester would say what he did, but he no longer had any doubts that his boy had joined those others in throwing tomatoes at him. At first he thought Sheriff Wolcott had said that only to get a reaction out of him so he'd act crazy in court, but he knew Bert wouldn't tell the sheriff that Lester was involved unless it was true. He thought back on how Lester had acted when he tried questioning him on whether he had heard any-thing—how Lester gave him a cock and bull story about some boy he didn't know the name of telling him it was a group of strangers from out of town. He remembered the way Lester looked when he told that story, and he knew Wolcott was telling the truth. It made things easy in a way. As far as he was concerned Bert was now his only son, which meant he didn't have to do anything to make sure that Bert would take over as the next Caretaker. He felt some relief accepting that, but it also pained him. He had hoped for better things for Bert.

He tried to clear his head and not think about anything except what he needed to. It was getting late, and he had to finish his day's weeding before the Aukowies grew any high-er. Still, as he made his way onto the intersecting path lead-ing to the field, he couldn't keep from chuckling as he pic-tured the look on Wolcott's face when he sandbagged him in court. It was the first time Jack Durkin could remember ever telling a lie, and he was amazed he was able to do it as bald-faced as he had, but what else was he going to do? There was nothing in the contract against it, and if he were put away for seventy-two hours, that would be it. Even if he were released after that it would be impossible to weed a field of three-foot-tall Aukowies.

He was still a hundred yards from the field when he heard their rustling. A breeze was blowing, but their rustling was more frenzied than what that breeze could've explained. When he got to the field both the breeze and their rustling stopped. He could see all of their little evil faces regarding him. For the first time in over three hundred years they had been allowed to grow unabated for hours, and he could sense the Aukowies' anticipation as they tried to decide what to do next—play possum or show their true colors. Caution won out, and they remained completely still as Jack Durkin resumed his weeding.

It was hard with a third of the field filled with five-inch Aukowies. He had to move carefully among them and use a trowel to hold them back while he pulled them out of the ground. At their height, if he wasn't careful, they could strike out and reach above his glove and slice his hand off at the wrist. It was tedious, back-breaking work, and he was exhausted by the time he finished the second pass of the field. He moved slowly, trying to straighten up and work the soreness out of his back and shoulders. Looking out over the field, he saw a new wave of Aukowies already growing tall. He picked up the canvas sack and carried it to the stone pit. After the sack was empty, he stopped to catch his breath and wipe sweat from his eyes. The Aukowies covering the first two-thirds of the field were aleady almost back to five ines in height, and stared at him with mixed anticipation and indecision. Durkin felt a tightening in his chest as he realized how hard the last pass of weeding was going to be. He stopped off at the shed so he could get the spade. When he started weeding, a groan escaped from him as he fought back the first dozen Aukowies.

The final pass took most of the night, and the last few hours had to be done under the light of the full moon. When he was finished, Jack Durkin stood motionless for a good twenty minutes before he was able to move. Slowly, he massaged the cramping in his arms and legs, then heaved the canvas sack over his shoulder and dumped the Aukowie remains with all the others. He put a match to the pile. The fire shooting out came close to singeing him and he fell backwards onto the ground barely escaping being burned, the flames exploded a good fifty feet up into the air. The only thing he could think of to explain the intensity of the fire was that most of the Aukowie carcasses in the pile were twice their usual size.

He sat quietly and watched the flames light up the night's sky. The stench from the burning Aukowies was worse than any time he could remember. Over the years he had gotten used to that smell, but this time he found himself pinching his nose. After the fire extinguished itself, he dusted himself off and buried the ashes. Then he headed home.

It had been so quiet at the field that it was a shock when he was a half mile or so away from it and heard crickets chirping and other critters scurrying about. If he listened, he could hear an owl off in the distance. Also coyotes. The only sounds he had heard for all those hours at Lorne Field was the blood rushing through his head.

It was after four in the morning when he reached his front door, which gave him less than two hours before he had to head out to the field again. He stopped inside the doorway and tried to get his work boots off, but it was a struggle with the way his feet had swollen up and how sore his back felt. When he was finally able to pull them off, he hobbled to the kitchen and tapped half a dozen aspirin into his open palm. He chewed the aspirin slowly. They reminded him how sour and empty his stomach felt. There was still leftover pot roast in the refrigerator, but Lydia's threat about what she'd do if she thought he intentionally cut off Lester's thumb stood out in his mind, her words flashing brightly as if they were on a neon sign. He dumped the leftover pot roast down the disposal, and instead poured himself a bowl of cornflakes and ate it at the kitchen table. Afterwards he filled up a bucket of hot water, shook in some Epsom salts and sat in the living room where he soaked his feet and dozed off and on.

The morning sunlight woke him. He shivered as he took his feet out of the bucket of now cold water and pushed himself out of his worn imitation-leather recliner and onto his aching feet. He made his way to the kitchen and chewed on another half dozen aspirins then, without much enthusiasm, poured himself another bowl of cornflakes. When he was done eating, he hobbled out to the front door and struggled to get his work boots on.

While he'd never admit it to her, it hurt him that Lydia didn't show up at the courthouse. It also made him feel funny inside knowing that she believed Lester's statement to Wolcott—or at least believed it enough for her not to call Hank Thompson. He thought that had to be why she didn't call Hank, that Wolcott must've spoken to her before she got around to it. The idea of facing Lydia's wrath was more than he wanted to deal with after spending a night fighting back a field of five-inch Aukowies, but he decided he needed to let her know that he was still alive and kicking. He let his work boot drop to the floor and made his way upstairs to their bedroom.

When he saw the empty bed and the open dresser drawers he realized what had happened. He didn't bother checking whether the drawers were empty. Instead, he walked back downstairs, forced his work boots onto his grossly swollen feet and set off to Lorne Field as required by his contract.

Chapter 8

The Aukowies seemed aware of the schism that had occurred the previous day in their death struggles with Jack Durkin and all the Caretakers before him. It wasn't anything Durkin could put his finger on, just a vague sense of dread. Maybe it was the way they stared at him, as though they were expecting something. They still mostly played possum, not putting up much more of a fight than usual when he ripped them from the ground. But all day he had trouble shaking an uneasiness deep in his gut that things had changed. He felt himself dragging, his bones feeling like they'd been filled with lead and his muscles with rubber.

When he got home that evening he realized for the first time that his car was gone. He tried to remember whether he had seen it that morning and decided he hadn't. Lydia must've taken it when she left the other day. He didn't bother pulling his work boots off at the door. Without Lydia there to harp on him, why bother?

There were still a couple of beers left from the six-pack Charlie Harper had brought over. He drank one of them while he searched through the refrigerator. There wasn't much in there, and he didn't feel like having cornflakes for a third straight meal. He hated the idea of imposing on Charlie after eating at his bar only a few nights earlier, but he rationalized that a cheeseburger, fries and a beer weren't too much to ask for breaking his back all day to keep Charlie and his family alive. In any case, he needed to bring him back his broken camcorder, and that night was as good as any to do that.

With his car gone, Durkin checked the attached garage his pa had built forty years earlier and found Lester's mountain bike stored inside. It was different than the kind of bike he was used to. He couldn't sit straight up on it, instead had to lean forward and put tension on his already sore shoulders. It was also hard getting the thing going, especially since he had Charlie's camcorder wrapped around his right wrist. He tipped over a few times, but after a half hour or so he got the hang of it. Not that he ever felt comfortable on the bike, but at least he was able to get the thing moving.

It was eight miles from his home to the center of town. When he got off the bike in front of the Rusty Nail, he could barely lift his arms, and his legs were so shaky he doubted whether he'd be able to walk more than a few feet. He lowered himself to the pavement and sat on the curb to rest. He heard cars passing him and could sense them staring at him as they drove by, but he kept his eyes cast down towards his feet. If they wanted to think he cut off Lester's thumb, that was their business.

When his legs felt less shaky, he got to his feet and entered the Rusty Nail in a stumbling shuffle. Charlie was working the bar. He nodded to him with an odd sort of look on his face. Durkin nodded back. He grimaced painfully at the bar stools, decided he had little chance of getting himself up on one and instead made his way to one of the empty tables. Charlie came over a short time later with a pint of beer. He handed it to Jack and stood awkwardly by the table wiping his hands on his bar apron. A strained smile showed on his large broad face.

"Can we talk a minute?" he asked.

Durkin nodded. "Sure. I need to talk to you anyway about your camcorder. Lester dropped it the other day when he was recording one of the Aukowies in action. I think he might've broke it. If you can figure out how much it costs to fix I'll pay you, otherwise I'll buy you a new one."

Charlie picked up the camcorder and examined it. "It doesn't look like it's turning on," he said.

"No, it don't."

"Maybe it's still covered by the warranty. I'll check." He sighed and waved the issue away. "Don't worry about it. You said Lester was recording one of the Aukowies in action?"

"Yep. I let one of them grow to a foot high. It's the reason he dropped the camcorder. When the thing shot out at me, it startled him."

"You have this on videotape?" Charlie asked, anxiousness tightening his mouth.

Durkin took a sip of his beer and shook his head. "I would except Lydia took the tape out of it before I left to the field."

"Why'd she do that?"

Durkin took another long drink of his beer. His eyes glazed over as he thought about his answer. "Because she thought I was going to make a fool out of myself and embarrass the family trying to prove that the Aukowies were nothing but weeds."

Charlie's face deflated. He nodded to the chair opposite Durkin. "Mind if I join you?" he asked.

"Nope, not at all."

Charlie pulled the chair out and perched uncomfortably on it. "That's an awful shame Lydia did that," he said.

"Yep."

"I heard about your son. About his thumb…"

Durkin nodded. "One of the Aukowies bit it off."

Charlie's mouth fell open and he gawked at Durkin.

"Saw it with my own eyes," Durkin said.

Charlie closed his mouth. He nodded dully and rubbed the knuckles on one of his large raw hands. "The story going around is he's claiming you cut his thumb off," he said.

"It ain't the truth, though. I know that's the story Sheriff Wolcott was telling in court, but it ain't what happened."

Charlie stared back down at his hands as he continued rubbing his knuckles. "Why'd you think Lester would say that?"

"I don't know. But it ain't true."

"I hear Lydia's got a cast on her hand."

Durkin took a sip of his beer and didn't say anything.

"I also hear she moved out on you."

"Did you hear where she moved to?"

"No."

"Well, she wasn't home last night, so I guess you heard right."

"What's with the cast?"

"I think she broke her hand."

"How'd that happen?"

"She got mad and hit the table. I didn't hurt my wife, if that's what you're asking."

Charlie kept rubbing his large thick knuckles. He looked up at Durkin and met his stare. His eyes were pale blue glass. "Why'd she move out, Jack?"

"You'd have to ask her."

Charlie let go of his knuckles and put his hand behind his neck as if he were feeling for bumps. "How about taking me to that field?" he asked.

"I can't do it, Charlie. I'd like to, but I can't."

"I hear others have been up there."

"They have, but not 'cause of me. I can't violate the contract. Things just get harder when I do."

"Five minutes, Jack. That's all I'm asking."

"Chrissakes, I can't. I'm sorry."

Charlie's face screwed up as if he were going to argue, but instead he pushed himself to his feet. "I understand," he said. He didn't look directly at Durkin. "I better get back to the bar." He hesitated. "How about some food? You want anything?"

"A cheeseburger and fries?"

"Sure. No problem."

When the food was ready, Charlie brought it over with another beer. This time he didn't stop to talk. Just gave a polite nod.

Durkin tried watching the ballgame on TV, but his mind floated too much for him to follow it. One minute a batter would be up, the next he'd either be on base or heading back to the dugout, and Durkin would have no idea what had happened in between. It was as if slices of the game were disappearing on him. When he was done eating, he left the bar and pedaled home on Lester's bike. Later, when he was on the sofa, it took almost ten minutes to pull his work boots off, and after he did, he soaked his feet and tried not to think of anything, especially the looks he caught out of the corner of his eye all night from Charlie.

That night he dreamt of his pa. He was back in high school, the night after his baseball team's championship game. He almost won the game single-handedly, hitting two homeruns and a double and making several tough plays at third, but his team still lost 8-7. His pa missed the game like all his other games since he had to spend the day weeding Aukowies, but in the dream they had dinner together and afterwards he came up to the bedroom that Jack shared with his brother. His pa asked Joe to leave so him and Jack could talk alone.

"I'm sorry I couldn't be there today."

"I know, pa."

"Your ma was telling me you almost carried your team on your back today."

Jack was in the middle of oiling his glove. He wiped off some of the oil and rubbed what was left deep into the leather.

"My last at bat I was slow to the ball," he said. "If I'd picked up on the spin faster I would've driven the ball over the fence instead of bouncing it off it. We would've won the game if I'd done that."

"Sometimes it's a matter of inches, son."

"Yep."

His pa sat silent for several minutes. Jack kept rubbing the oil deeper into his glove.

"Folks are saying you could be a big leaguer," his pa finally said.

Jack shrugged.

"I'm sorry, son," his pa said. "If it was up to me I'd make Joe the next Caretaker instead of you. But I can't do it."

"I know, pa."

"Everything in the contract's written for a reason. Any of us start messin' with it and we're all lost."

Jack nodded and kept his eyes on his glove. He tried hard not to cry. He didn't want his pa to see him crying.

"I know it ain't fair," his pa said. "I know it as well as

anyone, son. But if I made Joe the next Caretaker, then what happens if he has two boys? Neither of them are going to want the job when the time comes. And they'll have every reason to fight about it because I cheated with you. And then what? I can't set that type of precedent, son, no matter how much I'd like to."

"You don't have to explain, pa."

"But I want to. Nothin' I'd want more than to see you have a chance playing professional ball. But if we start cheating on the contract, we got big problems. We have to follow the contract to the letter. This thing is bigger than you or me, Jack. Ain't no job harder. You got the weight of the world on your shoulders. But you can do it, son. I got no doubt that you got it in you to be Caretaker. And as hard as the job is, people here will respect you for it. You'll be saving their lives every day. It makes it easier knowing that. Most days it's what keeps you going."

The sixteen-year-old version of Jack Durkin in his dream nodded and wiped a finger across his eye, trying hard not to let his pa see that he was wiping away a tear.

Durkin woke up and realized he was crying in his sleep. He was ashamed of it, even though there was no one there to see it. He wiped a hand across his eyes, then lay in bed thinking about his dream. He tried to remember if he ever had had that talk with his pa and decided he hadn't. He couldn't even remember his pa ever eating dinner with them. It was just a dream, nothing more. His pa never talked to him about playing baseball. Never acknowledged that he was all-state or had set state records with both his twenty-two homeruns and .620 batting average. The only talk he could remember having with his pa about something other than his future as Caretaker was after his freshman year of high school. His pa suggested that he drop out of school since there was no point in continuing.

As he lay in bed thinking about his dream, he realized it was the first time in years that he had thought about his pa. It had been almost thirty years since the old man died. After he had retired as Caretaker, he moved to Florida and only five years later dropped dead from a stroke. The funeral took place in August, and because it was held where his pa had retired in Bradenton, Florida, Durkin couldn't attend. It always bothered him that they couldn't have held the funeral back home, but he understood why. After so many years of weeding Aukowies, his pa wanted to spend eternity as far away from Lorne Field as he could.

Jack Durkin peered at the clock until his eyes focused. It was only two thirty-seven in the morning. He closed his eyes again, hoping he'd be able to get some more sleep. It was the first dream he could remember having since he was maybe five or six years old, and he hoped it would be his last.

❦

The next four days Jack Durkin didn't know what else to do but to keep going back to the Rusty Nail for dinner. He had no other food left at home, he had no money and he didn't even know what bank Lydia kept their money at—and even if he did, assuming there was still even any money in their account, he wouldn't be able to get there during business hours. Each time he went back to the Rusty Nail, Charlie's attitude seemed cooler. That fourth day Charlie asked him about Sheriff Wolcott sticking his hand into a clump of Aukowies.

"I heard he did that," Charlie said, his voice strained. "How come they didn't bite his fingers off like they did Lester's thumb?"

"'Cause they didn't."

"That's not a good enough answer, Jack."

Durkin peered at Charlie and saw the hostility brewing over his old friend's face. The muscles bunched up along the bartender's neck and shoulders, the same as if he were about to throw a drunken troublemaker out of his bar.

"Because they knew they could cause me more trouble by not doing anything," Durkin said.

"You're kidding. That's your explanation for it?"

"It's the truth, Charlie. I could see it in their faces. Somehow they knew."

Violence passed over Charlie's face like a storm cloud. He stood clenching and unclenching his fists, but the violence mostly petered out.

"According to Sheriff Wolcott they're nothing but weeds," he said, his voice tight. "Unless you've got cash to pay for your food and drink, you better leave."

Durkin left. When he got home he sat listening to his stomach rumble and tried to figure out what to do. He couldn't think of anything else, so he called Hank Thompson.

"Jack, how are you holding up?" the attorney asked on hearing Durkin's voice.

"Not so good." Durkin hesitated, feeling sick to his stomach having to beg this way. "I don't know if you heard, but Lydia left me."

"No, Jack, I didn't hear. I'm sorry."

"I don't know what to do, Hank. She took the car. I have no money and no food in the house. I don't even know what bank she uses. If I can just make it another seven weeks or so until first frost, I can straighten everything out then—"

"Jack, not another word. How about I drive over and pick you up. There's an all-night supermarket out on Route 30."

"I hate putting you out like this, Hank."

"It's no bother, Jack. Just hold tight and I'll be over soon."

Twenty-five minutes later Hank Thompson pulled his Cadillac into the dirt driveway. When Durkin got in the car, Hank offered him a handshake, then pulled the car onto the road leading away from the cabin.

"Must be quiet in there with Lydia and the boys gone," Hank said.

"I'm used to quiet."

"Still a shame for this to have to happen. Jack, I'll be deposing Lester next week. I'm hoping to shake the truth out of him so we can get him and Bert back home. Maybe if that happens Lydia will follow."

Durkin didn't say anything.

Hank cleared his throat and mentioned that the sheriff was spreading it around town that the only thing growing in Lorne Field were weeds. "He claims he stuck his hand in a bunch of them and nothing happened?"

Durkin felt a tightening in the pit of his stomach. He nodded miserably.

"Any idea why they left his fingers alone?"

"I don't know. I wish they had bit them off."

Hank laughed uneasily at that. "So do I," he said. "At least his pinky finger. Not that I wish too much ill will on our good sheriff, but it would make things easier for us. I've got a confession to make, Jack, and I hope it doesn't make you mad. When I was twelve I snuck down to Lorne Woods and watched your grandpa weeding them."

"You saw what they were then."

Hank nodded. "They weren't weeds. I can't say why, exactly. It's nothing concrete I can put my finger on, but I knew watching them that they were something other than weeds. And when your grandpa pulled them out of the ground, I swear I could hear something. Kind of like this shrill noise, almost what you'd expect from a dog whistle, but I'm positive I heard it."

"Their death cry," Durkin said.

"That's what you call it? I thought that sound was going to make my ears bleed. Anyway, it's always bothered me that I violated the contract. I apologize for that, Jack."

They drove in silence for the next ten minutes or so, then Durkin told the attorney why the Aukowies resisted biting off Wolcott's fingers. "I don't know how they knew they could cause more harm for me, but somehow they did."

Durkin looked over and saw the belief in the older man's face. He swallowed back a sob and bit down hard on his tongue to keep any more from coming up.

"If my grandpa had known he would've skinned you alive," Durkin said. "But that was a long time ago. The statue of limitations must've run out years ago."

Hank laughed good-naturedly. "That's *statute* of limitations. But thanks for the absolution, Jack. It's kept me up nights hoping none of you ever fell sick and couldn't weed that field. I lost many a night's sleep during my lifetime over that transgression."

Hank pulled into the supermarket's parking lot. Once inside he told Durkin to load up his cart with whatever he wanted. "Only a small payment for services rendered," he said.

As they went up and down the aisles, Durkin chose frugally, adding to the cart only the cheapest cans of baked beans, sardines, tuna fish and hotdogs he could find. Hank shook his head watching him.

"Christ, Jack, that's no way for a grown man to eat," he said. He brought a reluctant Durkin over to the meat department and had the butcher select several pounds of sirloin steaks, lamb chops and pork loin. Then he did the same at the deli counter, loading the cart with roast beef, ham, salami and an assortment of cheeses. After that he added packages of baked goods. When they checked out the bill came to well over a hundred dollars.

"When I get my affairs straightened out I'll pay you back," Durkin told the attorney.

"Absolutely not," Hank said.

They drove silently back to the Caretaker's cabin, but it was a comfortable silence. Hank helped him bring the grocery bags inside, and at the door when he was leaving, told Durkin not to worry about a thing and that he would call him after his deposition with Lester. Later, when Durkin was unpacking the groceries, he found two hundred dollars tucked in one of the bags.

The next week Durkin's spirits were as good as they'd been in years. Having a cupboard and refrigerator stocked full of food was a big reason for it, but an even bigger reason was not having to ride Lester's mountain bike into town any longer. It was bad enough that a day of weeding Aukowies left his muscles aching and his feet killing him, but the last thing he wanted to do after that was get on a bike and pedal for an hour so he could beg for food at the Rusty Nail. He was grateful he no longer had to do it. Accepting Hank's charity didn't seem nearly as bad, mostly because the older attorney believed in what those Aukowies were. Hank Thompson didn't have any doubts, unlike the rest of them. It was a relief not having to ride into town so he could see doubts—or in some cases outright disgust—creeping onto faces when the townspeople saw him. It was a blessing to simply be able to go home after his weeding, eat dinner and soak his feet. While it was quieter in the house than he'd like, he was comfortable by himself. Maybe at times he'd find himself missing Bert and, to a lesser degree, Lydia and Lester, but he found the emptiness of the house peaceful. At least he didn't have to see his own family doubting him, or worse, acting as if he were a joke.

A week after Hank had taken him food shopping he got a call from Hank that Child Services was delaying the deposition. "It's probably going to be pushed back another couple of weeks," the attorney told him. "Nothing to worry about, Jack. Just red tape, that's all. Child Services can be a real pain in the ass."

It was ten days after that call—a Monday—that Jack arrived back at the cabin after a day of weeding Aukowies to find boxes and furniture stacked up on his front yard. A padlock had been put on the door. There was also a notice nailed to it. In the early dusk, it was hard to read. Durkin had to strain to make out the single word **SEIZURE** that was printed in larger letters than anything else. He gave up and searched through the boxes until he found a flashlight. Then he went back and read the notice, read how the town council had terminated the Caretaker position and that the cabin and all associated lands were being seized by the town. If Durkin or anyone else entered the house they'd be arrested for trespassing. He read the damn notice half a dozen times before his anger subsided enough for him to think over the situation.

How in the world can I keep weeding that field now? he thought. *What am I supposed to do?*

He sank to the ground, his mind and body numb.

It struck him then that he was no longer bound by the contract. Not if the town was going to cancel it. Which meant for the first time in his life he was free. But free for what? To live aimlessly for the next eight days while the Aukowies grew out of the field and matured? And then to watch the world end?

It wasn't his concern anymore, he told himself.
He was no longer Caretaker.
Best of all, it would no longer be his fault when the world comes to an end.

That thought left him dizzy. It would no longer be his fault. He no longer had to carry the weight of the world on his shoulders. He was absolved. Free. If the town could turn their back on him, why couldn't he do the same?

But the world would still come to an end, regardless of whose fault it was.

Lydia would still be chewed up by the Aukowies, her small, hard-as-nails body turned into mincemeat. The same would happen to Bert and Lester. And every other living creature.

With a leaden heaviness weighing down his heart, Durkin realized it didn't matter that they turned their backs on him. The field still needed to be weeded. The world still needed to be saved. And that responsibility fell on him.

He sat for a few minutes sorting out his thoughts. After making up his mind about what to do next, he unpacked the boxes looking for his contract and the Book of Aukowies.

He went through all of the boxes without finding them, which didn't surprise him since whoever packed up the house had no clue about his hiding place in the basement. He did find his wallet in one of the boxes. It had been packed away since he never took his wallet with him when he weeded Aukowies. There was no point in doing that. He wished he had when he opened the wallet and saw that the two hundred dollars Hank Thompson had given him was gone.

It would be so damn easy to just turn my back on them. So damn easy . . .

But as much as he wanted to, holding his empty wallet before all those boxes scattered on his front yard, he couldn't just walk away.

The food from his refrigerator had been packed in a couple of the boxes and left in the sun to spoil. He sniffed the salami and sliced American cheese, decided they were still okay, and made a sandwich. He ate it slowly, then found the container of milk, sniffed it also, and poured out the spoiled contents. Fortunately, Hank had added a case of soda to his shopping cart. Jack Durkin found a can in one of the other boxes and drank it. When he was done with his dinner, he got to his feet and walked around to the back of the house.

When Durkin left that morning the back entranceway to the kitchen was covered by a screen door and an almost equally flimsy wooden door. The outer door's paneled windows would've been easy to punch out so the door could be unlocked. Both doors had since been replaced with something solid, and a padlock and seizure notice were attached to it. Jack Durkin hit this newer door with his fist several times and saw that he had little chance of breaking through it. He walked around the house sizing up his windows and settled on one in the kitchen. He broke the glass, cleared it away and used several of the boxes as a makeshift stepladder. The phone and cord had been packed away in one of the boxes. He took them with him, along with the seizure notice that he ripped from the back door, and crawled through the window.

It was awkward getting his thick body turned around and onto the kitchen countertop, and worse to lower himself to the floor, but he did it without cutting himself on any of the glass he'd broken. He turned on the lights. With the kitchen emptied out and all of Lydia's clutter removed from the countertops, the room looked small and foreign to him. He plugged the phone into the jack and heard a dial tone and was thankful they hadn't cut off phone service yet.

He called Hank Thompson and told him that his house had been seized.

"Whoa, slow down, Jack, tell me again what's going on."

"I came home today from weeding and found everything I own on the front yard with a padlock and notice on the door. According to the notice, the town council cancelled my Caretaker's contract and had my house seized."

"Do you have the notice nearby?"

"Yep. I can read it to you."

"Please do."

Durkin read the attorney the seizure notice. When he was done, Hank's voice sounded unnaturally tinny as he told him that the town had no right doing this. Durkin realized this was the first time he had heard Hank Thompson scared.

"They have to notify you first, Jack. They can't just storm into your house like Gestapo agents. This is America, for God sakes. It's not right. I promise you I'm going to get to the bottom of this. Wait a minute . . . Jack, where are calling from?"

"My kitchen."

"You're inside the house?"

"Yep."

"That's not good, Jack. You don't want to give them any excuses to arrest you."

"They left the Caretaker's contract in the basement. I'm getting it."

"Okay, I understand," Hank said, sounding almost panicked. "Get your contract as quickly as you can and leave the house. I'll head over there now and meet you out front."

Hank Thompson hung up.

Durkin took a step towards the basement steps and then wanted to kick himself for not bringing the flashlight in with him. He thought briefly about going back outside for it, but the thought of crawling out and then back in again through the window changed his mind. He left the basement door wide open hoping that enough light would filter down so he could see, then headed down the steps.

The light from upstairs didn't help much. By the time he got a few feet into the basement it was too dark to see anything. When he reached the back wall he tried to find the loose stones by memory, but pulled on half a dozen wrong stones before he found the ones that slid out. He could feel the book and contract in their hiding place. He took both of them out and headed back upstairs.

Durkin did a quick walk through the house to make sure nothing else was left behind. After satisfying himself, he went back to the kitchen, turned off the lights, and maneuvered himself so he was kneeling on the countertop and could lower himself out the window. Facing the kitchen, he put one foot out through the window, felt for the stack of boxes outside and steadied himself before sticking his other foot out.

"You're trespassing, Jack. I could arrest you for that."

Wolcott's voice startled him and he lost his balance and did an unintentional stutter-step off the box. He landed awkwardly, rolling over his left ankle and dropping the contract and Book of Aukowies. Wincing, he grabbed his injured ankle. He gritted his teeth and told the sheriff he had to go back into the house to get his belongings.

"We packed everything of yours up," Wolcott said.

"You left my contract and book in the basement," Durkin forced out through a clenched jaw. With horror, he saw that the binding for the Book of Aukowies had split open when it hit the ground and its pages were scattered around him. He fought back a sob. Hell if he'd let this son of a bitch see him cry. He gathered up the pages and placed them back in the book.

"You had no right doing what you did," he said. "No right at all."

"I had every right, Jack. I only did what the town council ordered me to do."

"You had no right. Dumping everything I own on my front yard. Not even giving me a day's notice."

"Jack, a notice was placed in your mailbox over a week ago. It's not my fault you're too busy saving the world each day to read your mail."

Durkin looked away from his injured ankle and into the placid face of the County Sheriff, who was staring him down as if he were nothing more than the town drunk. Durkin had never hated anyone more. He was overwhelmed with the thought of letting the Aukowies develop so that Wolcott and his family could experience their full horror.

"You're enjoying this," he said.

"No, I'm not, Jack. While I'm happy we're no longer wasting taxpayer's money on this nonsense, I've got to be honest and tell you that I find your situation sad. But, Jack, you've got no one to blame for this but yourself. You could've kept this gravy train going for years."

"Gravy train?" A sour laugh escaped from his lips. "Eight thousand dollars a year for breaking my back every day from spring thaw to first frost is a gravy train, huh?"

"Eight thousand dollars plus a free house. You conveniently left that out, Jack. And besides, eight thousand dollars for doing absolutely nothing is a lot of money. If you wanted to play the part in this charade and break your back, that was your business. And you know, Jack, if you just quietly did your weeding, the town would've kept this charade going. But you couldn't do that. You had to cut your son's thumb off, and God knows what you did to your wife. We had one lone hold-out in the council, but the final straw was seeing your wife walk out on you with her hand in a cast. Of course, your own words from the court transcript didn't help you."

Confusion mixed with the hatred in Durkin's stare.

"Don't you remember, Jack? What you said in court a couple of weeks ago? Where you admitted you're simply pulling out weeds everyday and that the town were saps for paying you to do that? I got a copy of that for the town council. It helped them make up their minds."

Durkin pushed himself to his feet, hobbling gingerly on his injured ankle. His hands clenched to fists at his side. Wolcott noticed his hands and the slight smile on his lips tightened.

"You knew I was saying that only for the benefit of the judge."

"You were sworn to the truth, Jack. Under threat of perjury."

"What if the truth is that there are creatures growing in that field? What then?"

"It's not the truth, Jack. If you really think that, then it's nothing more than a psychotic delusion on your part."

"What if it ain't? What if everything I've been saying is the truth?"

Wolcott took a step back, his hand resting on his service revolver. "A lot of what-ifs. What if Santa Claus were real?"

"If he was, the world wouldn't come to an end 'cause of it."

The sound of tires on the dirt road out front stopped them. A car door opened and shut, followed by Hank Thompson's voice bellowing about what an outrage this was.

"We're back here, Hank," Wolcott called out.

Hank Thompson was seething as he joined them. He pointed a long quivering finger at the sheriff. "You had no right doing this," he accused, his voice loud and booming.

"Calm down, Hank. I had every right. Besides, I was only following the directives of the town council."

"To sneak into my client's house and dump all of his belongings out in the street?"

"They were put out on his front yard."

"You know damn well what I meant. And don't you dare smirk at me!"

Wolcott held out a hand to stop the attorney.

"Calm down," he ordered. "I wasn't smirking at you. And as I was telling your client, a notice was sent over a week ago. There's nothing I can do if he chose to ignore it."

Hank's eyes slid momentarily towards Durkin, then

back on Wolcott with renewed intensity. "I'll calm down when I damn well want to. What if it was raining?"

"It's not."

"But if it was you would've still dumped everything he owned on the front yard?"

"Look, Hank—"

"This was wrong. Legally and morally you had an obligation to make sure my client was aware of the seizure notice and eviction plans."

"Which is exactly what I did!"

"By serendipitously placing a notice in the mail so it can be lost and never delivered?"

"By hand delivering it myself. I put it in your client's mailbox a week ago!"

"You had to sneak here and hide it in his mailbox? You didn't have the common decency to deliver it by hand?"

Wolcott shook his head. "I did what I was required to."

"Hank," Jack said, interrupting his attorney in the middle of shaking his finger again. "I found my wallet packed away in one of the boxes. It was empty. The two hundred dollars you gave me was taken from it."

The attorney shot a withering look at Wolcott.

"Hank, you know as well as I do that I only supervise packing up the house. Besides, it's your client's responsibility to pay attention to the seizure notice and make sure the house is vacated. If he fails to do so, then any lost property is his fault."

"I demand that you investigate this!"

"Come on, Hank—"

"You failed to properly notify my client, and assuming you didn't take the money yourself, two hundred dollars was stolen out from under your nose—"

"Be careful what you're saying, Hank."

"Not only that," Durkin interjected, his voice not much more than a croak, "they packed up the food from the refrigerator and left it out in the sun. Half of it's spoiled."

"Alright, alright," Wolcott said, flashing Durkin a look before staring angrily at the older attorney. "I'll look into this. But you know, Hank, your client broke a window and trespassed into the house. I could arrest him right now."

"He was retrieving personal property that you didn't bother to pack up."

"I made sure that nothing was left behind!"

"He had several items of great sentimental value that were hidden in the basement. If you'd like, I'm sure Jack will show you where they were."

Wolcott looked slowly from Hank to Jack Durkin. "No, that won't be necessary," he said. "It doesn't matter. Your client criminally trespassed, regardless of what might've been left in the house." He removed a pair of handcuffs from his belt and stepped forward. "I am placing him under arrest. You can accompany us down to the station house if you'd like."

"I'll tell you what," Hank Thompson said, his voice shaking with indignation. "If you do this I will sue you for abuse of power. Trust me, Sheriff, making your life hell will be my life's work. Maybe at the end of the day, you'll also get to find out what it's like to have your home seized."

Wolcott hesitated, then reluctantly slipped the handcuffs back on his belt. "I want your client off this property now," he said. "And all his junk too. Anything still here by tomorrow morning will be carted off to the town dump."

Hank sniffed dismissively. "Jack will be given a reasonable amount of time to remove his property. If you touch any of it he will sue you. Make no mistake about that, Dan. Now why don't you get the hell away from here and let me talk to my client in private."

Wolcott nodded. "Just make sure your client doesn't enter the house again."

"What about the garage?" Durkin asked.

"What?"

"My pa built that garage."

Wolcott stared at Durkin as if he sprouted horns.

"You'll have to bring that up with the town council," he said, his voice strained. "Maybe they'll let you move it to somewhere else. That's up to them. But I'm coming back here at midnight and if you're camped out anywhere on this property, I'm arresting you."

"Dan, let me ask you something," Hank said, his tone softer and more congenial. "You used to be a good kid, and were for the most part a nice guy as sheriff. When did you become such an asshole?"

Wolcott flinched as if he'd been slapped. "I'm only doing my job, Hank."

"A little too zealously, if you ask me. What do you have against Jack?"

"Other than cutting off his son's thumb? How about the way he's treated his wife." Wolcott pushed his hand over his scalp. "Mrs. Durkin looks twenty years older than a woman her age has any right to look. And now I see her walking around town with a cast on her hand. How'd that happen, Hank? I'll give your client until six tomorrow night to remove his property. Just make sure he does."

Wolcott nodded dully at them as he walked away. Hank Thompson stood stone-faced watching him. After the sheriff was out of sight, he sighed and turned to Durkin.

"Why the hell is Dan so fixated with Lydia?" he asked.

"She used to be babysit him."

"It looks like he's still carrying an adolescent crush on your wife. If I remember right, Lydia used to be quite pretty when she was younger. Jack, you didn't ever abuse her, did you?" Hank asked, his eyebrows arching slightly.

"Never once laid a hand on her. And as far as yelling goes, she always gave worse than she got."

Hank chuckled sympathetically. "Pretty much how I'd imagine it with her. I don't want to rub salt in the wound, Jack, but I doubt our good sheriff would be so gung-ho right now carrying out this eviction if Lydia hadn't walked out on you. Any chance of you two reconciling?"

Durkin frowned as he considered it. He stumbled, and when he tried to regain his footing, ended up putting weight on his injured ankle. Wincing, he sat down quickly.

"Are you okay, Jack?"

"I hurt my ankle coming out of the window. I hope it ain't broke."

"Jesus."

"I think I'll be okay. I just need to sit here for now. About what you asked, unless Lester changes his story she ain't moving back with me."

Hank lowered himself to the ground and joined Durkin.

"What a mess," he said.

"Yep."

"It explains why Child Services has been putting me off. Must be someone on the town council having them do that. They probably didn't want to risk Lester recanting his statement until after your eviction. Well, Jack, I'm just going to have to push harder for that deposition."

Durkin didn't say anything. He was too choked up at

that moment to say anything. He dusted dirt off the Caretakers contract and handed it to Hank.

"This is the contract?" Hank asked. The attorney held it at arm's length to take a look at it but it was too dark to read it.

Durkin nodded.

"I'll go over this carefully tonight," Hank said. "With your family occupying this house for several hundred years this contract could amount to a land grant. It amazes me they thought they could get away with this. But then again, with some of the newer town residents on the council they probably didn't believe that this contract even existed. Don't worry, Jack, I'm going to get you back in that house."

Durkin nodded dully as he examined the Book of Aukowies. Tears welled in his eyes.

Hank put a hand on his shoulder. "That's the book?" he asked.

"Yep. It's been in my family over three hundred years. The binding split open when I fell."

Hank took the book from Durkin and looked through the pages. In the dusk he could still make out the drawings of the Aukowies.

"This is what they look like fully grown?"

"Yep."

Hank's face grew even more gaunt as he stared at the pictures. He closed the book.

"Jack, the binding can be replaced. Leave the book with me and I'll get it fixed."

"Thanks. I'd appreciate it."

"Least I can do, Jack. I'll get it done right away."

The attorney picked himself off the ground and gave Durkin a hand to help him to his feet. He looked at Durkin with concern.

"I should take you to the emergency room," he said.

"Nope. It's probably just a sprain. Anyway, I got too much to do."

The two men started towards the front of the house, Durkin in a badly hobbled gait and Hank walking slowly to keep pace with him. The concern on the attorney's face deepened as he watched the way Durkin moved.

"You need to get that ankle looked at."

"Not tonight," Durkin grunted.

Hank offered to put Durkin up at his home when they reached his car. "You can stay with me until we get this mess resolved, or if you'd like, tomorrow I can find you an apartment."

"How far away is your new home?"

"It's only the next town over. I'd say no more than fifteen miles from here."

"I can't do that." Durkin shook his head, his jaw locked in a determined scowl. "I need to stay close to the field."

"Jack, I can drive you back here anytime you'd like."

"Nope. Wouldn't want to put you out that way. Besides, I got other plans."

"Jack, really, it's no bother…" Hank Thompson stopped as he stepped back on his heels. He froze for a moment, then tapped his chest. "Indigestion," he told Durkin. "I shouldn't have had that extra helping of stuffed cabbage." He smiled weakly as he took out his wallet and peered inside it. He counted what he had and handed the money to Durkin.

"Forty-three dollars," Hank said. "All I have on me. If I knew those bastards lifted the two hundred dollars from you, I would've stopped off at an ATM before coming here. You're sure you're going to be okay?"

Durkin nodded without much conviction.

"Call me tomorrow," Hank said. "I'm going to fix this, Jack, I promise. I'll be filing an emergency injunction tomorrow morning to get you reinstated as Caretaker and back in your house. Don't worry about a thing, Jack, we've got a valid contract on our side." The attorney sighed as he gazed at the boxes and furniture scattered across the front yard. "It might take a few days to get all this worked out, so I'll arrange to have your belongings put in storage. I don't want to give our good sheriff an excuse to throw your property away."

"I appreciate all this, Hank."

The attorney fixed Durkin a careful look. "Are you sure you're going to be okay?" he asked.

"Yep. I'll be fine."

The attorney took Durkin's hand. His face grew a shade grayer as he stared more intently at Durkin. "You're sure you're going to be able to weed that field tomorrow?"

"I'll take care of it."

"Okay, Jack." Hank lowered himself into his Cadillac. "If you need anything you call me, understand?"

The attorney showed a comforting smile as he held up the Book of Aukowies and promised Durkin he'd get it repaired. As he pulled away, he honked his horn and waved out the window. Durkin watched until the car disappeared around the bend. Then he found his flashlight and hobbled painfully to where he'd left Lester's mountain bike.

Chapter 9

In retrospect, Jack Durkin could've planned better. Not that he had much choice in the matter. The idea of staying with Hank Thompson gave him the willies. While he liked Hank and felt comfortable around him, Hank's wife was another matter. Jeanette Thompson was a tall willowy woman, about the same height as her husband and with the same thick cigar-ash colored hair. Originally from Manhattan, she had gone to the same ivy league college as Hank, and the few times she met Durkin, she had looked at him as if he was nothing but a specimen in a jar. Even more importantly, he had spent every night of his life at the Caretaker's cabin, and the thought of being an overnight guest in anyone else's house was strongly distasteful to him. But it was more than that. He couldn't be dependent on anyone to get him to Lorne Field in the morning. Still, after spending three hours in the dark, first riding Lester's mountain bike back to Lorne Field and then pushing a wheelbarrow from the shed to the Caretaker's cabin, hobbling every step of the way on an injured ankle, he wished he had come up with a different plan. He also wished he had found the aspirin before he left.

He pushed the wheelbarrow over to the boxes and nearly fell over when something large crawled out of one of them. He turned his flashlight on it and saw four raccoons digging into the box.

"Git out of there!" he yelled.

The raccoon nearest to him arched its back and hissed. The others ignored him.

"I said git!"

This time all the raccoons ignored him.

Durkin picked up a stone and threw a fast ball hitting the nearest raccoon in the ribs. It let out a loud hiss, turned towards Durkin, then changed its mind and scampered off. Durkin zipped a couple of more stones at the other raccoons and they followed, disappearing into the nearby woods.

He hobbled over and saw the box they were digging into was one of the ones with perishable food packed into it. He pushed it away and found the boxes with the canned goods, then loaded the cans into the wheelbarrow.

"Almost forgot the can opener," he muttered to himself. "A lot of good those cans would do me without it."

Durkin searched through more boxes until he found the can opener. The same box had the family silverware, and he grabbed a fork and spoon. He went through the rest of the boxes and loaded blankets, sheets and a pillow into the wheelbarrow, along with a small suitcase that he packed most of his clothes into.

In one of the boxes he came across a plaque naming him the state's most valuable baseball player his freshman year of high school. He had forgotten about the plaque. He probably hadn't seen it since the night he was awarded it at the celebration dinner. He lingered for a moment looking at it, and then dropped it back in the box.

He was pushing the wheelbarrow away from the cabin and onto the path to Lorne Field when he saw flashing lights approach the house. He checked his watch and saw it was a couple of minutes to midnight. The idea of Dan Wolcott checking his garage and house to make sure he wasn't there infuriated him, but he was too damn tired to do anything but trudge forward.

When he was two miles away from the cabin he remembered that he had forgotten the aspirin again. He thought about turning back, but decided if he did he'd never make it back to Lorne Field by morning.

Jack Durkin tried setting up some bedding on the floor of the shed, but couldn't stand the cramped quarters. Boards from the wood floor dug into his back and it was unbearably hot and stuffy. After a while, he realized there was no reason he couldn't camp outside instead. It wasn't raining, and no bugs or critters came within a half mile of Lorne Field. He pulled the blankets and sheets and pillow outside and set up behind the shed so he wouldn't have to see the field. It was completely still out there. No crickets chirping, no insects buzzing, absolutely nothing but a dead quiet, interrupted only occasionally by the groans that accompanied his restless movements. He wished to hell he had remembered the aspirin. He also prayed his ankle was only sprained and not broken. As it was he left his work boot on his injured foot. He knew if he took it off he'd never get it back over the ankle in the morning.

Earlier he had organized the food he brought, and if he was careful he would have enough for three weeks. First frost was four weeks away. Maybe it would come early. Whatever happened, he wanted to be prepared to last the season in case things dragged out with Hank's litigating.

Once he was camped outside, he could only sleep fitfully for a few minutes at a time before either the hard ground or his ankle woke him. At one point he got up and loosened the

ground with the spade. It didn't help. Within minutes of
tossing and turning, his weight packed the ground hard
again. He'd have to stop by the Army Surplus store the next
day and see if Jerry Hallwell could loan him an air mattress.

After a few hours he couldn't take the hard ground and
his throbbing ankle any longer and slowly rolled onto his
knees. Using the shed for support, he pulled himself to his
feet. He tottered for a moment, and grimaced as he tested
his ankle.

The sun was hours from appearing in the sky. It wasn't
quite dark, wasn't quite light either. More of a murky gray-
ness. Looking through it was like looking through a fog.
Jack Durkin squinted at his watch and saw it was only four
twenty-nine. He hobbled past the shed and looked over the
field. It was completely dead, and it would probably be
another couple of hours before the first wave of Aukowies
pushed their way through the dirt. He stood transfixed by
the emptiness of the place and the eerie stillness of it. After
a few minutes, he turned away from the field and made his
way into the shed. He opened a can of baked beans and ate
it cold for breakfast. Then he waited until the Aukowies
appeared.

The day of weeding was the hardest he ever had to
endure, even harder than the two weeks when he had pneumonia. Maybe it was because of his injured ankle, but he felt
feverish and all day alternated between sweating profusely
and shivering in the eighty-five-degree heat. He was only
able to complete two passes of weeding with each one
taking over seven hours. The Aukowies sensed that he was
injured. He could see their indecision as they were torn
between playing possum or acting more boldly, but they
chose to keep playing possum.

He couldn't carry the canvas sack on his back. Once the weight of the Aukowie remains reached twenty pounds, the canvas sack would collapse him to his knees. He ended up having to cart it around in the wheelbarrow.

He had started weeding early—as soon as the first wave of Aukowies broke through the field—but it was still after sundown before he finished the second pass. He looked over the field and saw small Aukowies covering the first half of it. He decided to let them wait, that he'd start early the next morning and get to them then. After he burned the pile of Aukowie remains and buried their ashes, he ate a can of sardines and wearily mounted Lester's mountain bike and headed towards town in the hopes of obtaining an air mattress from Jerry Hallwell's store.

It was past ten by the time he reached the town center. The Army Surplus store was already closed for the night, as was the town drugstore. Somehow he'd have to leave the field earlier the next day so he could get an air mattress. Earlier when he had passed the Caretaker's cabin he saw that his belongings had been taken away as Hank had promised, so if he wanted aspirin he was going to have to ride out to the all-night supermarket. Every muscle in his body ached, and his ankle hurt to the point where he was fantasizing about chopping his foot off. He needed aspirin badly, and he needed to sleep on something other than hard ground.

He dialed Hank on a payphone outside the town drugstore. As the phone rang he thought about Hank's offer to put him up. He found himself wondering again about that offer. Maybe one night wouldn't be so bad...

Hank Thompson's wife answered the phone and curtly asked who was calling.

"Hello, Jeanette, this is Jack Durkin. I know it's late, but can I speak to Hank?"

"No."

There was a sharp click as she hung up.

Durkin stared at the receiver befuddled. Even though he had recognized Jeanette's voice, he still couldn't help wondering whether he had dialed a wrong number and talked to someone who only sounded like her. He dug out change from his pocket for another call and tried Hank's number again. On the third ring Jeanette answered, a chill coming from her voice as she demanded to know who was calling.

"Jeanette, I know it's late and I apologize," Durkin said, his words tumbling out in a rush. "But I know Hank's expecting me to call—"

"My husband's dead," Jeanette Thompson said. "He died last night from a massive coronary, in no small part due to the agitation your hysteria caused him."

She hung up the phone again.

Durkin took several steps away from the phone, dazed, and then stumbled back to it. He searched his pockets, found enough change for another call and dialed Hank's number again. When Jeanette Thompson picked up, he told her how sorry he was about Hank. "Your husband was a good man," he said. He stopped for a moment to collect his thoughts. On the other end there was only a stone-cold silence.

"I know this is bad time to be asking this," he said, "but Hank had things of mine that are important. A contract and a book. I need to get them back—"

"Yes, Mr. Durkin," she said harshly, "this is a bad time for you to be asking me for anything. I saw my husband die last night. I spent today arranging his funeral. If you want those items returned, call me back in a week, and if they haven't been disposed of, I will see that they are returned to you. If you call back before then I will make sure those items are thrown in the trash."

She hung up again.

Durkin took several steps away from the payphone and sat down on the curb with his head in his hands. He had never felt more lost. He sat for a long moment, wondering how he was going to save the world without Hank's help and cursing himself for letting the contract and Book of Aukowies out of his possession. But what difference did it make? Let her throw it away. He was no longer Caretaker, so what difference did any of it make?

He thought of his pa and his grandpa before him. How weeding that field turned them both into old men before their years. How they were both in their early fifties when they died, only a few short years after retiring as Caretaker. He thought about how much they had sacrificed of themselves. He thought about how much he himself had sacrificed.

There was a reason for all of it.

He steeled himself and fought against the despair crashing down over him. What he did was too important to let his feelings overwhelm him.

He was going to get his contract and book back from Jeanette Thompson. He was going to finish this season and weed those damn Aukowies until first frost. After that he'd have all winter to talk sense into the members of the town council. He knew that he'd have to get Lester to come clean and tell them what really happened before they changed their minds. Later, after this season of killing Aukowies, he was going to find Lester and get through to his son.

Jack Durkin wiped his hand across his eyes and then pushed himself to his feet. The streets were mostly empty. If anyone had driven or walked by, he hadn't seen them. He hobbled over to his bike and walked it to the Rusty Nail.

❧

Charlie Harper stood impassively as Durkin hobbled into his bar. After Durkin laboriously seated himself on one of the stools, he ordered a shot of bourbon, defiantly meeting Charlie's cold stare.

"Three dollars," Charlie said.

With some difficulty, Durkin worked his wallet out of his back pocket, took out a ten dollar bill and placed it in front of him. Charlie stared at the bill for a good minute before picking it up and holding it to the light to make sure it was genuine. Satisfied, he put the bill in his pocket and poured Durkin a shot of bourbon.

"Where's my change?"

Charlie had moved down the bar to pick up some empty glasses. Without looking at Durkin, he said, "It's costing me forty bucks to fix the camcorder that you broke. I'm making those seven dollars a down payment towards that, and I expect the rest of the money later."

"You'll get it," Durkin said. "Every penny of it."

He lifted up the shot glass and stared at the amber liquid. Silently he said a prayer for Hank Thompson's soul, then downed the bourbon in a single gulp. For a few seconds, the burn of it made him forget the throbbing in his ankle.

He cleared his throat and told Charlie that the town council had cancelled the Caretaker position. "That means the contract's no longer in effect as far as I'm concerned, either," he added. "If you want to come down to that field with me I'll show you what those Aukowies really are."

Charlie was wiping a rag over part of the bar. He froze, his muscles tensing. All at once he started laughing an angry laugh.

"Is that so," he said.

"Yep, it is. What's so funny about that?"

"Nothing. It's pathetic, that's what it is." Charlie walked over to the cash register and took out a folded up newspaper that had been shoved underneath it. He unfolded the paper and placed it in front of Durkin.

"I've been saving this in case you ever had the nerve to step back in here," he said.

The page in front of Durkin had an article about his arraignment hearing from a few weeks earlier with the headline '*I'm Only Pulling Out Weeds Everyday*'. The gist of the article was that he had come clean in court and admitted that the legend of monsters growing out of Lorne Field was nothing but a hoax so that he, and his ancestors before him, could milk it for all it was worth. Durkin's face reddened as he read the article.

"I only said what I did because the judge needed me to," he insisted.

"Sure, that's why you said it."

"If I didn't I might've been locked up in jail. And then there'd be no one left to weed the Aukowies!"

Charlie eyes glazed over as he stared at Durkin. He didn't bother to respond.

"Christ, Charlie, just come to the field with me, then! I'll show you firsthand what Aukowies are!"

"I've got a better idea," Charlie said. "Why don't you go

peddle your bullshit elsewhere. And unless you want to buy another drink, get the hell out of my bar."

Durkin opened his mouth to argue, saw the hardness settling over his former friend's face, and instead lowered himself from the barstool and did as Charlie suggested.

Chapter 10

Over the next ten days Jack Durkin left Lorne Field only twice—once to try calling Jeanette Thompson, the other time so he could go back into town and ask Jerry Hallwell for an air mattress. That was the day after he found out about Hank, and he caught Hallwell locking up his Army Surplus store, but Hallwell turned him down flat. One look at Hallwell's face told him that he had read the same newspaper article as Charlie Harper and, like Charlie, believed every word of it.

"I can take you down there, Jerry," Durkin told him. "You can see for yourself."

"Take me down there? What for, so you can cut off my thumb like you did your son's?"

Durkin watched helplessly as Hallwell turned his back on him.

After that night, the idea of leaving the field exhausted him. Even when he ran out of aspirin he couldn't get himself to mount Lester's bike and ride the six miles to the supermarket for more. So when he finally finished the day's work, he'd eat a dinner of either cold beans, sardines or tuna fish, drink a can of soda, and sit leaning against the shed until he thought he might be able to doze off for a couple of minutes. Then he would lay down on the three blankets he'd brought and try to ignore the aching in his back and the sensation of nails being hammered into his injured ankle and a constant fever that kept him shivering uncontrollably. Even when he'd fall into unconsciousness for a minute or two from sheer exhaustion, his clattering teeth from the now cooler nights would wake him.

It was around noon the following day when a rattling noise coming down the path to Lorne Field interrupted Durkin from his weeding. He looked up and was surprised to see his son, Bert, on his bike. He croaked out for Bert to stay where he was, his voice not much louder than a hoarse whisper.

Bert had gotten off his bike and started to approach the field. Durkin motioned with his arms and yelled at him again to stay put. He shuffled as quickly as he could on his injured ankle towards his son. He could see the worry on Bert's face over his appearance. He hadn't washed, shaved or bathed since he had been evicted from his home. From the way his shirt and pants hung loosely on him he knew he'd lost plenty of weight. When he reached Bert he stood awkwardly, not sure what to do.

"I'd hug you, son," he said, "but I know I must smell pretty bad."

Bert stepped forward and buried his face into his father's chest. Durkin stood with his hands at his side for a moment, and then embraced his son.

"I've smelled worse," Bert said.

"I don't believe that for a second."

"Well, maybe not, but I've missed you, dad."

"I've missed you too, son." Durkin took a step back so he could see his son. Bert was trying hard to smile but couldn't stop looking worried.

"Where are they keeping you?" Durkin asked.

"In a foster home over in Eastham. If they knew I did this I'd be in big trouble," he said, his grin turning sheepish.

"Eastham? That's a long way from here. At least twenty miles."

"It took me all morning to ride my bike here," Bert said, now proud of his crime.

"You ain't supposed to see me, huh?"

Bert shrugged noncommittally.

"What's this foster home like?"

"It's okay." Bert looked down and kicked at the dirt. "Lester's there with me. All he does all day is try to play video games with one hand and look at dirty pictures on the Internet."

"Son, I didn't hurt your brother. Whatever he's saying, it ain't the truth."

"I know, dad. Lester's a weasel. He only said that stuff because he doesn't want to become Caretaker."

"What makes you say that?" Durkin asked. "Lester tell you that?"

"No, he doesn't tell me anything anymore. But I know what a lying weasel he is. And that's why he said those things."

Durkin looked away from his son and towards the Aukowies growing in Lorne Field. "When you see Lester you tell him to tell the truth. He don't have to be Caretaker."

"I will, but I don't know if it will do any good."

"Just tell him." Durkin took a deep breath. "Why don't I show you how to weed them. You can help me."

"Sure, dad."

Weeks ago when Durkin had gone through the boxes left on the front yard of the Caretaker's cabin, he found an extra pair of work gloves and brought them with him. Now he asked Bert to go back to the shed for them. Bert did as he was asked. The gloves were several sizes too big for him, and given how thin and slight Bert was, they made him look like a cartoon character. Almost like Mickey Mouse. But they would do. As they walked back to where the Aukowies were growing, Durkin took short, shuffling steps, trying hard not to grimace. He could feel his son's eyes on him. He turned towards Bert and smiled, the questions plain on his son's trusting face. About the way he was walking and how he was sweating so profusely and the fever that was burning brightly on his face and how thin and emaciated he had become.

"I'm okay, son," he said. "Just a couple more weeks of weeding and first frost will be here. I'll be able to rest then."

They walked quietly to the waiting Aukowies. "Stand back, son," Durkin said. "If you look carefully you can see their little faces. When they're bigger, there's no mistaking those evil grins of theirs. But even now you can see them."

"I-I think I can see it," Bert said.

Durkin pointed a finger at the nearest one. "Right there, see the way it's looking at us. It's hoping we'll think it's just a weed, but it's watching us. You can see its little slit-eyes and grinning mouth and horns. You see it, Bert?"

"I see it, dad."

"Listen to the sound it makes when I kill it."

Durkin pulled the Aukowie from the ground and then looked hopefully over at Bert. "You hear it?"

"I-I'm not sure. What's it supposed to sound like?"

"They scream when they die. Sometimes it takes a while before you're able to hear, but just keep listening for it."

"Try another one, dad."

Durkin pulled another Aukowie out of the ground.

"I heard it," Bert said, his eyes focused off into the distance, his brow furrowed in concentration. "I heard it scream."

Durkin felt proud as looked at his son and knew he was telling him the truth. It brought back memories of the first day his own dad had taken him to Lorne Field. "Kind of what you'd imagine a dog whistle would sound like if you could hear it," he said.

"That's exactly how it sounded!"

"You want to help me, son? You can push the wheelbarrow while I weed them."

"Sure, dad."

"Now, don't be alarmed, but I'm going to get on my knees. It's just easier for me that way right now. My back's been hurtin' a little, and so's my ankle, but it's nothin' serious."

Durkin got down on all fours and started pulling out Aukowies and handing them to Bert so he could put them in the canvas sack. "Be careful how you hold those. Even though they're dead, the fangs on them are razor sharp."

"I'll be careful."

As Durkin weeded, he explained to Bert how he felt for the right angle on the Aukowies so they'd come out easily and not break off in the ground. Looking at his son's face, he knew Bert was picking it up.

"I'm going to be the next Caretaker, won't I, dad?"

"I'm afraid so," Durkin said, his voice growing even more hoarse. "There's no way around it."

"I don't mind."

"I know you don't, son," Durkin said. He wished that there was some other fate possible for his boy. He could feel the weight of his son's future pushing down hard inside his chest. Without looking at Bert, he asked if he'd seen his ma.

"She's trying to get us back with her," Bert said softly. "She visits every other day with a social worker."

"Where she's living?"

"Mom's got her own apartment."

Durkin turned a questioning eye towards his son, but muttered that that was good. "You know how she's able to afford it?" he asked.

"Her friend, Mrs. Vernon, helped her. Mom's going to be writing a book."

Durkin backed away from a patch of Aukowies and stared hard at Bert. "That ain't possible," he said. "She talks even worse than I do. That woman can barely read, let alone write. What in the world could she be writing a book about?"

"Someone's going to be helping her. They're paying her a lot of money to write about her life."

Durkin could see the real answer in his son's embarrassment. "You mean about how she's married to a crazy loon who thinks he pulls out monsters from a field all day long and cuts off his son's thumb?"

Bert shrugged, his grin weakening. "I don't know, dad."

"It don't matter," Durkin muttered. He went back to his weeding. "Good for her. Let her take them for every penny they got."

Durkin let his son help him for another half hour, then with a grunt pulled himself to his feet and smiled sadly at him.

"You better be headin' off," he said. "You got a long bike ride ahead of you."

"I can help you some more."

"No, I don't want you riding your bike in the dark." He winked at his son. "Or gettin' in trouble at that foster home. Just tell Lester he needs to come clean. And tell your ma I'll be talking to her soon."

"I will." Bert looked away and kicked at the ground. He

stuck his hands deep in his pockets. "Dad, when I rode by the house I saw a padlock and eviction notice on the door."

"It's just temporary, son. Nothin' to worry about."

"Where are you living?"

"I'm camping out here until the season's done." He winked again at his son. "It's fun. Playing Daniel Boone, livin' out here in the wilderness."

"Why don't I stay with you and help?"

"Can't do that, son. It would just get you in trouble. And me, too, when they come lookin' for you. But I'll be seeing you soon. Three weeks at the most, I promise."

He held out his hand, and Bert looked at it, his bottom lip quivering. He stepped forward and grabbed his father in a hard embrace. Durkin stood helplessly for a moment, then embraced his son and smoothed the hair on his head while whispering hoarsely to him that everything was going to be okay. He let go after a minute, telling his son he had to get back to his weeding. Bert nodded glumly and took a step away.

"I started school already, so I can't come during the week, but I'll be back next Saturday," he said.

"You better not. It's too long a ride. Besides, you'll just get yourself in trouble."

"Nope, I'm coming back." Bert walked reluctantly towards his bike. He stopped to wave to his father. "I'll see you next week!"

Durkin waved back and watched as his son got on his bike and rode away. After that, he went back to his weeding.

Bert didn't come back the next Saturday.

Durkin thought about it and decided the bike ride must've been too much for the boy, or maybe someone at the foster home had found out about his first trip to Lorne Field and took his bike away. Twenty miles back and forth was a lot of riding, and he couldn't blame Bert for not doing it again. In a way he was glad he didn't. He didn't want his boy seeing him the way he was; besides, he'd have plenty of opportunities to see Bert after the weeding season was over. He had too much on his mind as it was. His ankle wasn't getting any better, his back was stiffer and more bent each day, and he kept thinking about his last phone call with Jeanette Thompson. As she had asked, he waited a week before calling her again. This time her voice was shriller than before, sounding like nails on a chalkboard. She told him that she couldn't find the items he had asked about and must've thrown them out. Before hanging up, she warned him not to call again, and that if he did, she'd take out a restraining order against him.

When he got off the phone he almost rode out to the town dump, but he was just too tired. As exhausted and near panicked as he was, he knew he'd have no chance of finding his contract and book buried in a mountain of garbage—that all he would accomplish would be getting bit up by rats. He decided that was probably what Jeanette Thompson wanted. It made no sense for her throw those items away, and she was probably just trying to work him up and send him on a wild goose chase as punishment for Hank's death.

Later, after first frost came, he would call her again and explain the importance of getting his contract and the Book of Aukowies back. Given a chance to calm down, she'd return them.

It was more than two weeks after Bert had showed up at the field that Durkin started hearing noises. It was low at first, sort of a mechanical rumbling sound, but every couple of hours or so it appeared to get louder. The next day he started hearing men's voices mixed with the mechanical rumblings, and the day after a bulldozer pushed through the path with a tractor following behind to roll over and flatten the ground. Both pieces of equipment stopped at the edge of the field. The driver of the bulldozer squinted hard at Durkin. "No one's supposed to be here," the man called out. He stepped out of the bulldozer and stood next to it with his hands on his hips, a baffled look on his face.

He was a square man with a pudgy face, who was either bald or had his hair cut close to the scalp—hard to tell which with the hardhat covering his head. Durkin didn't recognize him and guessed he was from out of town. He pushed himself off his knees and onto his feet. It took him some time to straighten his back and for his head to stop swimming.

"No one's supposed to be here," the construction worker yelled out to him. "Get off the field!"

Durkin surveyed what he had done so far. While he had two-thirds of the field weeded, he had started from the other end and the field between him and the two construction workers was covered with four-inch Aukowies. As the scene fully registered on him and he saw the sneakers that one of the construction workers wore, he knew if the man stepped into the field he'd have his ankles sliced to ribbons. Durkin almost turned his back on him, knowing that if that were to happen it would convince the town once and for all what the Aukowies really were. He couldn't do it, though. Sighing heavily, he tried waving the men away and yelled out in a voice that wasn't much more than a hoarse croak for them to leave. He could see it wasn't doing any good. The two workers just stared back at him with confused expressions screwing up their faces, one standing by the edge of the field, the other sitting on his tractor. Reluctantly, Durkin shuffled slowly over to meet them.

"You have any idea where you are?" Durkin asked. He peered at the man sitting on the tractor. He didn't recognize him, either, but saw that the worker had taken out a cell phone and was talking hurriedly into it.

"What? I don't know what you're talking about." The pudgy construction worker took a step away. Durkin saw the nervousness flash on his face and had a good idea what was behind it. He was afraid he was either dealing with a crazy person, or a contagious one.

"Ron," the man on the tractor yelled out to his co-worker, "I made a call. Let's just wait until some people show up, okay?"

Ron exchanged glances with his co-worker, then slowly backed up to his bulldozer and got into it. He sat with his arms crossed, his eyes small and piggish as he watched Durkin.

Looking at the way both men stared at him, Durkin could feel his temper slipping away. "You want to learn about where you're at?" he heard himself asking them. "Just stick your hands in those weeds and you'll learn all about Lorne Field." He started to move closer to the bulldozer, but Ron made a shooing motion with his hands. "Just go back to what you were doing and stay away from me," he said.

Durkin stumbled back on his heels, dizzy. He knew it was mostly his fever, a constant since hurting his ankle, but it was also partly not knowing what to do. He couldn't fight either of those men, not in the condition he was in. And even if he could, what would be the point? The one in the tractor had already called the police. They were going to come and remove him from the field like they did his home. Then these two were going to be left to do God knows what. He broke out laughing then. A hoarse, aching sound that hurt deep in his chest. He noticed their reaction to it and it only made him laugh harder. *So what*, he thought. *He was no longer Caretaker. This was no longer his problem. The hell with it. The hell with all of it.* He took a couple of short, shuffling steps away from the field, then froze, slumping, his knees turning to jelly under him. As much as he wanted to, he couldn't just walk away. Not with only a week or so before first frost. He had no idea what else to do, so he made his way back to the Aukowies and continued his weeding.

It didn't take long for Sheriff Wolcott to arrive down the dirt rode that the bulldozer and tractor had made. Wolcott stepped out of his jeep and started towards Durkin, who turned his head and saw with some disappointment that Wolcott was wearing boots. Durkin turned back to his weeding.

Wolcott walked up to Durkin and watched him silently. After a few minutes Durkin acknowledged him, muttering "*Sheriff*" half under his breath.

"Jack," Wolcott said. "I had no idea where you had gone to. Don't tell me you've been living out here all this time?"

"Ain't against the law, is it?"

"Well, yeah, technically it is. This is town property and trespassing notices have been posted. But forget that for now." He hesitated, his tongue wetting his lips. "Jack, we need to talk."

"Go ahead and talk. It's a free country. But I got weeding to do."

Wolcott stood silently for several more minutes, then in a quiet voice said, "You don't look well, Jack. It doesn't even look to me like you've been eating. How much weight have you dropped, forty pounds? Let me take you to the hospital. We can talk after you see someone."

"I've been eating fine. And I told you, I'm busy."

"You're no longer Caretaker, Jack."

"It don't matter. Somebody's got to keep saving the world each day."

Wolcott watched while Durkin pulled up another dozen Aukowies and then repeated that they needed to talk.

Durkin turned and looked at Wolcott through red-rimmed eyes. "You think I ain't nothing but a crackpot, huh? How about I prove to you what these Aukowies really are."

He pulled his work glove off his left hand and reached down into a clump of Aukowies. He had his eyes squeezed shut, waiting for them to tear his fingers off. He could feel them bristling against his skin, but nothing else. He opened his eyes and could see them weakening. They'd been waiting for this chance for years, and he knew the temptation was too much for them. He could feel the tension building in them as they struggled to keep from ripping him apart.

"Jack, what are you doing?"

"Just give me a minute," he forced out, his voice sounding like his throat had been scraped with sandpaper. "They ain't going to be able to hold out much longer. A little while longer and they'll show you their true colors."

"For Chrissakes, Jack, just stand up already!"

He felt the Aukowies rustling harder against his skin. He knew it was only a matter of seconds before they'd lose control, but before that could happen he was dragged to his feet. Wolcott had his arms around his chest and was lifting him up, and Durkin was too weak to fight it. He looked angrily in Wolcott's eyes and saw nothing but sadness.

"You arrestin' me, Sheriff?" he grunted out.

"I don't want to, Jack, but if you don't leave the field I'll have no choice. We do need to talk. It's important."

"What about?"

"This is not a good place, Jack—"

"You want to talk to me, talk now!"

Wolcott filled his lungs and let it out slowly. He looked away.

"There was an accident. Two weeks ago last Saturday. Your son, Bert, was riding his bike on the highway and he was hit by a truck. I'm sorry, Jack, but he didn't survive."

Jack Durkin's stare turned blank. Breathing heavily, he left the wheelbarrow and canvas sack where they were and started towards the new dirt road that had been built. Wolcott kept pace with him.

"Jack, if I had any idea you were out here, I would've sent someone for you."

Durkin continued to walk straight ahead as though deaf and dumb to the world. He went past the bulldozer and tractor and kept going. Both construction workers looked questioningly at the sheriff, who signaled for them to look away. Wolcott stepped quickly and grabbed Durkin by the elbow.

"Let me drive you somewhere. I can't just leave you like this."

Durkin ripped his arm free and kept his short shuffling pace until he reached the shed that his great grandpa had built. There, he stored his work gloves inside the shed, took Lester's bike and pushed himself on it. The bike tottered for a long moment as he pedaled. For a few seconds it looked almost as if he were on a stationary bike before it started to roll forward. Wolcott stood watching. When the bike was rounding the bend, he yelled out that if Durkin came back to the field he was going to have to arrest him, that he would have no choice.

Chapter 11

Jack Durkin bought a machete at the Army Surplus store for twenty-five dollars. Jerry Hallwell eyed him suspiciously as he rung up the sale.

"What are you buying a machete for?" he asked.

"Wha'cha think for? My weeding."

"I heard you weren't doing that anymore."

"You heard wrong. Put that in a bag."

Hallwell gave Durkin a long look before doing as he'd asked. Durkin handed him thirty dollars and Hallwell counted out the change.

"It looks like you lost a lot of weight."

"Special diet."

Hallwell nodded soberly. "I'm sorry to hear about Bert," he said.

Durkin's lips formed two grim lines as they pushed hard together, but other than that gave no indication he heard. He took his change and the machete and left the store. After buying some aspirin at the drug store, he took out what he had left from the money Hank had given him and counted six dollars and change. He chewed on a handful of aspirin, then walked across the street to the diner and took one of the booths.

When the waitress came over, he ordered scrambled eggs, sausage, pancakes and a pot of coffee. The waitress hung around looking uncomfortable. Durkin thought it was because of the way he looked and smelled, but then she started to tell him how sorry she was about what happened to Bert. He looked up at her and saw her smiling somewhat sad and brittle. She was young, no older than twenty, blond, and thin as a stick—maybe even skinnier than he had become. He saw her name tag read *Nancy Wilkens* and realized she was Lucy and Ed's little girl, all grown up.

"Thank you, honey," he told her.

She nodded, her smile growing sadder. "I used to see Bert riding his bike around town, always carrying his fishing pole. He was such a nice boy."

The muscles along Durkin's jaw hardened. He turned and looked out the window. After he felt her leave, he wiped the back of his hand across his eyes.

She brought the coffee pot first and he emptied it quickly, drinking six cups from it. She brought another pot with her when she brought the food. He had no appetite and barely tasted any of what he ate, but he knew he was going to need his strength. He knew he was going to have a hard night in front of him. He methodically finished what was on his plate, then sat back and drank more coffee. When the second pot was empty, Nancy came over and asked if he'd like more coffee or anything else.

"Nothing more, thanks," he said, trying hard to smile at her. "Just the bill."

"There's no bill, Mr. Durkin. This is on me."

"That ain't right—"

"No, please."

Jack Durkin took the six dollars and change that he had left and placed it on the table. "I can still leave a tip," he said, winking. Before she could argue with him, he pushed himself out of the booth and hobbled out of the diner.

Shayes Pond could've made a nice Monet oil painting, with the lily pads floating on the surface and willow trees scattered along the banks. Jack Durkin knew Bert liked to go fishing there, and more times than not would bring home fresh water bass that he caught from the pond. Like Bert, Durkin went fishing a lot when he was younger, usually at a spot he'd discovered at Crystal Pond, but he could see why Bert liked this place. Once Durkin took over as Caretaker, that part of his life was gone. He saved his fishing pole and gave it to Lester when he turned ten, but Lester never really had any interest in it, and eventually his prized fishing pole ended up in Bert's hands.

Probably because it was a school day, he had the place to himself. No other boys like Bert out there fishing. In a way he was disappointed. He found a grassy spot in the sun and sat down. For weeks he had heard nothing but his own moaning and sighing, but here he could hear bullfrogs in the weeds and squirrels and birds chattering noisily in the trees. The racket they made was soothing. It made him want to close his eyes, but he fought the urge. He had too much to think about. It was only three o'clock and he had hours to wait before it would be safe to head back to Lorne Field and deal with the Aukowies. There was still one-third of the field that he had never gotten to, and given all day to grow unabated that part would be covered by one-foot high Aukowies. He knew the Aukowies on the rest of the field would reach at least six inches high. Even at his strongest, he doubted whether he'd be able to handle the field like that. In his present shape, the only chance he had was using the machete.

He found himself staring at the pond and trying to picture Bert sitting on the bank with his fishing pole. After a while he gave in and let his eyelids close, then lay down on his back and felt the sun warming his face. Every time he'd start to drift off he'd think of Bert being hit by a truck and he'd be jolted awake. It got to where all he could see in his mind's eye was Bert's lifeless body.

He squeezed his eyes shut and rubbed them hard with the palms of his hands and tried to blot out that image.

What haven't I done for you? he thought. *What more do you need to take from me? I'm beggin' you, just tell me which one you're doing, punishing me or testing me? Which one is it?*

He cried then. Tears lined his heavily-weathered face, his chest aching with each sob. After a while his exhaustion caught up to him and he passed into something between sleep and unconsciousness.

It was dark when Durkin woke. Disoriented, he pushed himself into a sitting position. Slowly it came back to him and he remembered everything that happened that day. He remembered what happened at the field. He remembered about his son. He squinted hard at his watch and saw it was nine thirty-five. After chewing on some aspirin, he found the machete next to him, pushed himself to his feet and got on Lester's bike.

He rode first to the Caretaker's cabin, then onto what used to be the dirt path to Lorne Field. They had turned it into a dirt road wide enough for two cars. At the start of the path the town had posted a sign warning against trespassers and announcing that construction would be starting soon for a new subdivision of luxury homes. When he reached the field there was enough moonlight for him to see that the shed was gone. He searched further back in the woods from where the shed had been and found remnants of it there. Picking through the pile of broken boards, he found his flashlight, tested it to make sure it still worked, and walked back to the edge of the field and flashed the light over it.

It was as he expected it. At the end closest to him the Aukowies were a foot-high and swayed towards the light. It was a cool, crisp night, with the air dead still, but he could see them swaying. He could see their faces waiting in anticipation. His jaw muscles set, he took the machete and went to work.

An hour later he had made only a small dent in the field. He stopped to wipe the sweat from his face, then rested with his hands on his knees and waited for the pounding in his chest and temples to slow down. Off in the distance he could see headlights coming down the new dirt road. As Wolcott's jeep came closer, the headlights framed him. The jeep came to a stop with the engine still running and the headlights left on. Wolcott stepped out of it. The lights were bright enough that Durkin had put a hand to his eyes as he squinted towards Wolcott. Wolcott's face was left mostly in shadows.

"Is that a machete you're holding?"

Durkin was still winded from his exertion. He tried answering, but couldn't manage the breath necessary. Even buried in shadows, he could see the harshness on Wolcott's face.

"Damn it, Jack, put the machete down."

"Dan, I'm only doing what I have to. Why don't you go home and leave me alone."

"Put the machete down now! This is the last time I'm telling you!"

Wolcott's hand dropped to his service revolver. Durkin looked from him to the field of Aukowies.

"They dug up this field today, didn't they?" Durkin said. "At least enough for their road. How come if these are just weeds, they're growin' here as strong as ever?"

"I don't know, Jack, and to tell you the truth, I don't care. They're only weeds. That's all they are."

"If that's true, how about you stepping out among them? You do that and I'll drop the machete. Not only that, I'll never come back here. I promise on my son's grave."

"Damn it, Jack, if those were really monsters growing out there, don't you think the army would've been brought in, or something like that? You really think they would've left it to one man to protect the world?"

Durkin kept his gaze fixed on the Aukowies. "It's been done this way for a reason. Once Aukowies are given a chance to mature, bullets and bombs won't make much of a difference to them," he said. He could hear Wolcott swearing to himself. He kept his gaze focused where it was. He didn't want to look at Wolcott.

"Is that what it's going to take to satisfy you? Fine, Jack, I'll take a little stroll among your weeds."

Wolcott walked past him. Jack Durkin closed his eyes and covered both his ears with his hands. He didn't want to see what was going to happen next, and he certainly didn't want to hear it.

Chapter 12

It was forty minutes after Sheriff Wolcott was gone when Jack Durkin walked over to the Sheriff's jeep and shut off the engine. He knew he had no chance of cutting down the Aukowies with the machete, especially after they had tasted human blood. How much blood did a man's body hold? He remembered reading the answer to that when he was in school. What was it, something like six quarts? However much it was, the Aukowies had had all of it. No, the machete wasn't going to work anymore. Something else had to be done to kill them.

He flashed his light in the front seat, then the back and finally the trunk compartment before finding a water bottle he could use, but he couldn't find anything to siphon gas with. A Molotov cocktail would be easier, but there was another way he could do it. He looked around outside the jeep and found a rock that would be big enough, then dropped it on the passenger seat and drove the jeep to about twenty yards from the edge of the field.

The headlights of the jeep caught the Aukowies swaying in the night's air, still drunken from their feast. Durkin wished Dan Wolcott could've seen it. That sight would've changed his mind. But it was too late for that now. He went back to where the remains of the shed had been scattered, searched through the rubble and found one of his blankets. He brought it back to the jeep and used the machete to cut a strip widthwise from the material. After popping the trunk open, he used the dipstick to spread oil over the strip and then pushed it into the jeep's fuel tank. He got back into the jeep, started it, and waited until the cigarette lighter turned hot enough. He took the lighter and held it against the oil-coated fabric until it caught on fire. It burned slower than he expected—the blanket must've been treated with flame retardant chemicals—but because of the oil spread on it, it did burn. When it had burned three-quarters of the way up, Jack Durkin placed the rock on the gas pedal. The rock wasn't heavy enough to push it down much, but enough to where he could get the engine to rev up a bit. Reaching in, he put the jeep in drive. The jeep lurched forward, knocking the wind out of him and dragging him almost into the field before he was able to push himself out of it. Holding his ribs, he sat on the ground and watched as the jeep drove into the field and exploded. The blast knocked him over. He could feel the heat of it over his body. Then he could hear them screaming. Thousands of Aukowies burning to death, their cries piercing the night's air. He cupped his hands hard over his ears and tried to block out the sound. Rolling up, he could see the flames spreading over the field and shooting up into the sky.

The ashes were still smoldering when the police car showed up. He looked over his shoulder and saw Bob Smith getting out of the car. He turned back to watch the dying embers blinking red across the field. A light flashed on the side of his face. He heard Smith call out, asking if that was him. He didn't bother to respond. A minute later he could hear Smith breathing heavily out of his mouth. He looked out of the corner of his eyes to see Smith holding his nose.

"Gawd, it reeks here," Smith said. "I don't think I ever smelled anything worse. What did you do out here tonight?"

"Only what I had to."

"Did you see Dan Wolcott?" Smith asked. "I got a call from his wife. He was supposed to be heading out here a while ago, but he hasn't come home yet. She's worried."

"He was here," Jack Durkin said. "He's gone now."

The police officer was flashing a light across the field and it hit the burned out shell of Wolcott's jeep. The light froze on it.

"Oh my God," Smith said. "What did you do tonight?"

Durkin didn't bother to answer him. He just stood up and put his hands out in front so Officer Smith could cuff him.

❧

Jack Durkin was taken to the State Police Station in Eastham and put in an interrogation room and told to wait. It was many hours later when police detective Dave Stone came in and introduced himself. He was about Durkin's age, large-boned, with bloodshot eyes and a rumpled look about him. Along with a manila file stuffed under one arm, he carried a box of donuts and a tray holding two coffees into the room. He took a few sips from one of the coffees and slid the other over to Durkin and offered him a donut. Durkin looked blankly at both before shaking his head. He stared bleary-eyed at his watch until he could focus on it.

"It's nine-ten in the morning," Durkin complained. "I've been left alone here almost eight hours."

"I apologize for that," Stone said. He took another sip of his coffee and then a bite of his glazed donut. Brushing the crumbs from his lips, he added, "As you can probably guess, we've been busy. Now, Mr. Durkin, why don't you tell me what happened last night."

"I already told Bob everything."

Stone nodded agreeably. "I know you did," he said. "And we appreciate your cooperation, but why don't you tell me again so that I can hear it in your words."

Durkin stared hard at Stone's artificially friendly smile. He was sure the detective was struggling not to react to how badly he smelled. He knew full well he reeked with both the stench of burnt Aukowies and all those weeks outside by himself. *Fine with me*, he thought. *Let him suffer if he's going to keep me here all night like that.* He shrugged and took the coffee that had been offered to him. "You got cream and sugar for this?"

Stone took some sugar and cream packets from the cardboard tray and slid them over to Durkin, along with a plastic coffee stirrer.

"I ain't got nothin' different to tell you than what I told Bob Smith."

"Why don't you tell me anyway."

"I killed Dan Wolcott, just like I told Bob."

"That's the part I'm confused about when I read your statement. How'd you do it again?"

"Wolcott didn't believe me about the Aukowies. I challenged him to walk into the field. When he did they tore him apart."

"And that's how you killed him?"

"Yep." Durkin stared coldly at Stone as he drank his coffee. "I knew what they were going to do to him. He wouldn't have walked out there if it weren't for me."

Stone opened the manila folder and searched through the papers in it. He found the one he was looking for and skimmed his finger over it as he read it. Like Durkin, he had thick stubby fingers.

"And what about the machete?" he asked.

"What about it?"

"You didn't use the machete to kill Sheriff Wolcott and cut his body up?"

"Of course not."

"Mr. Durkin, we know you bought a machete yesterday from Hallwell's Army Surplus store. We found it at the field."

"I told you what happened."

Stone flipped through the manila folder and pulled out a photograph. He placed it on the table in front of Durkin. The photograph showed the lower part of a boot that had been cut off at the ankle. A severed foot was plainly visible inside the boot.

"We brought dogs to the field," Stone said. "They found this foot in the woods. It's Sheriff Wolcott's, isn't it?"

Durkin nodded softly as he stared at the photograph. "They must've flung it out there in their frenzy." He jerked his head up to meet Stone's red eyes. "You took dogs out there? I bet they wouldn't step foot in that field!"

"Why wouldn't they?"

"'Cause of the Aukowies growing there, that's why!"

Stone let out a heavy sigh. "There's nothing growing in that field."

"That can't be true."

"Mr. Durkin, I left there only a half hour ago. There's nothing there but ashes and a burnt out jeep. Your setting fire to the field did the trick. I doubt anything's going to be growing there for a long time."

Durkin sat back in his chair, a confused look spreading over his face. "That don't make sense," he said.

"Mr. Durkin, where's the rest of Sheriff Wolcott's body?"

"What?"

"I know you cut up Sheriff Wolcott's body and left his foot in the woods. I also know you did this because you wanted to be caught, the same reason you hung around waiting for Officer Smith to come by and arrest you. Mr. Durkin, for the sake of Dan's family, what did you do with the rest of his body?"

Durkin closed his mouth, his eyes vacant as he stared at the detective. "From this point on, I ain't talking to you without a lawyer," he said.

Jack Durkin was taken to the County Jail for processing. When the warden saw him, he immediately had one of his guards get Durkin a clean set of clothing. "You change into this," the warden told Durkin, putting the new clothes and a bag outside his cell. "Leave what you got on in this bag. We're going to have to throw your clothes away. No use trying to save them."

The warden came back a half hour later and saw Durkin frowning dourly as he sat on his cot wearing his new shirt but still wearing the same soiled and filth encrusted dungarees as before.

"How come you haven't changed your pants?" the warden asked.

"I can't get my work boots off."

"What do you mean you can't get them off?"

Durkin shrugged, his frown turning more dour. "I hurt my ankle a few weeks back and I can't get the boot off my foot."

The warden had one of the guards enter the cell to pull off the boots. When Durkin passed out from the pain, the warden decided he'd better have him taken to the hospital.

The emergency room doctor who cut off Jack Durkin's boot blanched when he rolled off the wool sock and saw the severely blackened foot underneath it.

"Your ankle's broken," he said in a voice that sounded too calm to Durkin. "When did you hurt yourself?"

"I don't know. Maybe four weeks ago."

The doctor told him he'd be back and then left to consult with the warden who had accompanied Durkin to the hospital. "This is a very sick man," he told the warden. "It's a miracle he's still alive. Along with being dehydrated, malnourished and carrying a high fever, he has one of the worst cases of gangrene I've ever seen. He needs to be admitted for surgery right away. How long has he been in police custody?"

"Since last night."

"He should've been brought here immediately. There's no excuse for this."

The warden made a face. "I agree. Jesus, the guy's nothing but skin and bones, and with the story he was telling them they should've realized he wasn't right. So what do you need to do to him?"

"We need to cut off his foot and get him on some serious antibiotics." The doctor left the warden to arrange for the emergency surgery. Twenty minutes later when Durkin was on the operating table, the anesthesiologist told him to count down from ten.

"Someone's got to weed that field," Durkin warned, his voice barely a whisper, his eyes rolling wildly.

"Please, just count down from ten."

By the time Durkin reached six he was out.

During the next three days, Durkin flitted in and out of consciousness. When he woke up, his fever had broken and he found his left wrist chained to the hospital bed and his injured ankle throbbing worse than ever. For a long moment he stared blinking, with no clue where he was. Slowly the cloud fogging up his head lifted a bit and he realized what was on his wrist, then he remembered where he was. He also knew that it must've been days since the Aukowies had been weeded. Unless first frost had come early, it was already too late.

A nurse came by a short time later and noticed he was awake. "You're finally back among us," she said, her tone flat, her eyes and mouth plastic and expressionless. "And how are you feeling?"

He tried to talk but his lips and throat were too dry for him to do anything but croak out a hoarse whisper. She held a plastic water glass for him so he could suck on the straw. With his lips and throat wetted, he tried to talk again and whispered that his ankle hurt.

"If you press the button next to you, you can control your pain medication," she told him.

Durkin reached blindly as he searched for the button. When he finally got his hands on it he pressed it several times. He caught her looking at him no differently than the way a snake might. "How come I ain't seen my lawyer yet?" he demanded.

"I'll let the doctor know you're awake," she said without emotion as she turned and left the room.

It was hours later when the lawyer from the public defender's office showed up. He looked like a kid, wearing a cheap suit that was two sizes too big, with a thick mop of unruly brown hair covering his head. He introduced himself as Brett Goldman and sat hunched over, grinning a lot, though he had trouble making eye contact. Durkin explained to him the history of Lorne Field, what happened that night with Dan Wolcott, and why it was so important for him to be let go. Goldman nodded regularly, grinning down at his hands as he rubbed them together as Durkin might if he wanted to start a fire with sticks.

"Why do they got to keep me chained to the bed like this?" Durkin complained bitterly. "With my foot cut off how the hell can I run off?"

"They have to, Jack. They're just following regulations."

"It's Mr. Durkin to you. And quit rubbing your hands like that! You're making me nervous."

Goldman gave a lopsided grin and moved his hands awkwardly to his sides.

"Sorry, Mr. Durkin," he said, sneaking a peek at his client before lowering his eyes. "I guess I'm a little nervous, too. Now, I've spoken to the doctor you saw when you were brought to the emergency room. He told me that you were a very sick man. Do you realize you almost died?"

"I realize I ain't got my foot no more. That's what I realize!"

Goldman smiled sympathetically. "I know, Mr. Durkin, and I'm truly sorry about that. According to Dr. Brennan you were very sick that day, and quite likely delusional. I know you think you know what happened at that field with Sheriff Wolcott, but the reality is that as sick as you were you didn't know what you were doing and you didn't know what you were seeing. We have a very strong case for temporary insanity."

Durkin sat quietly while the lawyer spoke, a deep scowl folding his face. "I ain't crazy," he said.

"I'm not saying you are." Goldman brought his hands together and absentmindedly started rubbing them together again. He caught Jack Durkin glaring at them and he shoved his hands into his pockets. "The important thing now is to get you released so you can go back to that field, right?"

"I know what I saw," Durkin said slowly, "I ain't delusional. And I ain't letting you say that I'm crazy."

"How about this," Goldman said. "You keep telling people what you saw and let me take care of the rest."

Durkin was going to argue with him that it was important for people to believe what happened, but the morphine and antibiotics had wiped him out. He sank back into his bed and closed his eyes. Before drifting off, he murmured to the lawyer to find out if first frost had come yet. That the fate of the world depended on him learning that.

Later that night Goldman was at a local brewery slowly working through his second nut-brown ale when he was clapped on the shoulder from behind. He turned with his lopsided-grin in place for William McGrale, the state's attorney who was going to be prosecuting Jack Durkin.

"Goldman, how'd you get in here?" McGrale asked. "Let me guess, you used a fake ID?"

Goldman shook hands with McGrale. "Nah, I threw my fake one out years ago. I've been legal six years now. How are you doing, Mr. McGrale?"

"After three scotches, pretty damn good." A slight sheen showed over the prosecutor's eyes. "What do you say you grab that soda pop you're drinking, and the two of us move over to a table and discuss your client."

"Are you buying dinner?"

"Anything for a deserving young attorney."

Goldman took his glass with him and followed McGrale to his table. When the waitress came over, McGrale ordered another scotch, Goldman another beer, along with a cheeseburger and onion rings.

"Maybe when you grow up you'll start ordering a big boy's drink," McGrale said, smiling pleasantly.

Goldman shrugged off the dig. "You realize that I have a strong temporary insanity defense," he said.

"And how's that?"

"Have you talked to his doctor? Durkin was at death's door when he was brought in. A hundred and two fever, gangrene throughout his foot and ankle. Shit, he was hobbling around on that broken ankle for four weeks, pulling out weeds because he thought if he didn't the world was going to come to an end. He was absolutely delusional, with no idea even which way was up."

"All that may be true, but juries hate the temporary insanity defense. All my years as a prosecutor, I never once saw a jury buy it."

"Forget temporary, my client's insane. It scared the hell out of me just sitting with him. And that was with him chained up!"

"He's as crazy as a loon," McGrale agreed. He stopped to take his drink from the waitress and offer her a smile. After she walked away, he studied his drink for a moment before sipping it and looking back at Goldman. "There's a big difference, though, between insane and criminally insane. No, Goldman, your client knew what he was doing. I don't know if you're aware of this, but there were charges filed against him earlier this summer for cutting off his son's thumb. I talked to Jill Bracken already about it. He did that solely as a ploy to convince that town of his that those weeds were monsters. Same reason he killed Sheriff Wolcott."

"And that's not insane?" Goldman asked.

"Not criminally insane, no."

The waitress came back with Goldman's food and ale and placed it in front of him. His grin was halfhearted at best as he picked up the burger and took a bite.

"I thought your office was floating the theory that my client blamed the sequence of events leading to his younger son's death on Sheriff Wolcott. That the murder was done for revenge," Goldman concluded decisively.

"A little bit of both," McGrale admitted.

Goldman considered this as he took another halfhearted bite of his food. "Mr. Durkin really does believe that monsters grow in Lorne Field," he said. "And not just him either. That town has been paying his family for over three hundred years to weed that field."

McGrale rolled the last sip of scotch around his mouth the way a wine connoisseur might do with a fine burgundy before swallowing it. "I heard something about that. Doesn't surprise me. They always seemed a bit inbred over there. But again, there's a big difference between insanity and criminal insanity. It all comes down to whether your client understood his actions, and he clearly did. As insane as his motives might've been, he fully understood his acts."

Goldman put his burger down so he could dip an onion ring in some ketchup. "Mr. McGrale," he asked. "What exactly do you want?"

McGrale held up a finger to the waitress to signal for another scotch before turning back to Goldman. "I have a family that's grieving right now," he said. "They want to bury their loved one, but they can't because there's no body.

If your client discloses where he hid the rest of Sheriff Wolcott, I can offer man-two, with a minimum of ten years."

"Quite a deal," Goldman said.

"Given what he did, I'd say so."

Goldman's lopsided grin showed again. He took a long drink of his ale and laughed sourly to himself. "I'll talk to him, but I don't think he's going to take it. I don't think he's going to let me plead insanity either. I think he's going to force me to argue that there are monsters growing in Lorne Field."

"There are ways around that. Have him declared incompetent."

"I could try to do that, but what if he's right?" Goldman said, his grin fading. "According to the forensics report there was no blood found on the machete."

"So?"

"Why cut off Sheriff Wolcott's foot and leave it in the woods, but wipe the machete clean? And even if he wiped it clean, there still should've been traces of blood found."

"Not necessarily," McGale countered. "There are chemicals you can use to remove blood traces."

"And how exactly would my client get his hands on those, living out there in the middle of that field? And what bothers me even more is the report that the foot was sliced and not hacked off. My client was deathly ill, his weight had dropped from one hundred and seventy pounds to one hundred and thirty in about a month, and yet he was able to cut off that foot with a single blow from the machete?"

"Ah, Goldman, you're making this so damn complicated. The insane can show amazing strength sometimes." McGrale held up a finger for emphasis. "But let me repeat, insane, not *criminally* insane."

Goldman let out a sigh. "I'll talk to my client tomorrow. If I have to get the ball started on competency hearings, I'll do it."

"That's fine, Goldman. Remember, though, I'm going to need the location of the body before I can agree to any deal."

Goldman shook his head and laughed softly to himself. "You realize how nuts this is? To go to court to prove my client is mentally incompetent, but still not criminally insane?"

The waitress brought McGrale another scotch. He smiled sadly at it, knowing he had reached his limit. "If our office's psychiatrist considers him criminally insane, I won't fight a lifetime confinement to one of our fine mental institutions."

Goldman finished his dinner, but stopped himself at three ales. He knew there were a number of police officers unhappy with him taking this case—as if he had any choice—who would be looking for a chance to pull him over for a DUI charge. After leaving McGrale, he sat in his car trying to make up his mind about something, then finally took out his cell phone and called his mother.

"Have we had first frost yet?" Goldman asked.

His mother sighed heavily. "I had just gotten into bed," she complained. "You're calling me at ten o'clock at night to ask me that?"

"Mom, please."

"Well, if you had your own garden you'd already know the answer."

"Well, I don't."

"Yes, I know, you're too busy as a hotshot lawyer to bother with a simple activity like gardening."

Hotshot lawyer. He wanted to laugh. Public defender

was nearer the bottom rung of the ladder, although this case could get his name in the paper. If it went to trial.

"Mom, please, can you just answer the question?"

"The answer is no. There hasn't been a frost yet. But I'll call you when we have one."

"Thanks."

After hanging up, he headed home. Before he had driven more than a few blocks, he turned his car around.

Goldman had left his car and was standing on the edge of Lorne Field. He had to admit that it was eerie standing out there under the full moon. The place had a desolate feel to it. No animal sounds, no birds or insects, nothing. That part of what Durkin had told him was true. But he also found himself disappointed that there was nothing growing there. The field was completely empty. Wolcott's burnt-out jeep had been removed and there was nothing there but ashes from the fire. It made sense that there wouldn't be any weeds growing there now, but it didn't stop his disappointment. Goldman walked out into the field and could feel the hairs standing up on the back of his neck. He hurried back to his car, his heart racing with irrational fear. He could only imagine what spending four weeks alone out here could do to a man's sanity, especially if you were already unhinged enough to believe that the weeds growing up where you slept were blood-thirsty monsters.

Chapter 13

The following morning Jack Durkin's lawyer nudged him awake from a morphine-induced sleep to tell him about the deal being offered. Durkin refused. "Even if I wanted to, I couldn't accept it," he said irritably. "There ain't no body. The Aukowies saw to that."

His lawyer hunched over and stared at his hands. "Well, I guess that answers that," he said. "Anyway, the state's psychiatrist is going to be evaluating you—"

"I told you, I ain't crazy!"

"I understand that, but the state has the right to order this, so I'm asking that you cooperate with her. Oh, by the way, I have good news for you." He tried to grin, but it didn't stick and slid off his face like a fried egg from a well-buttered frying pan. He lowered his eyes from Durkin's hollow ones and stared back at his hands tapping out a drum beat on his knees. "I got a call from my mom this morning. We had our first frost of the season last night. The world should be safe."

"Don't treat me like an idiot," Durkin said, his voice trembling. "I know you don't believe a word I've been telling you about the Aukowies. But you drive out there yourself and you'll see. Frost or no frost, they should be five feet tall by now, and somethin' has to be done about them."

Goldman continued to stare at his hands. "I drove out to Lorne Field last night. Mr. Durkin, there was nothing growing there."

"That don't make sense."

"The fire you set scorched the ground and covered it with ash. With those conditions, probably nothing will grow out there for a while." Goldman forced his lopsided grin as he peeked back up at Durkin. "Think of it this way, Mr. Durkin. You beat the Aukowies."

Durkin looked confused as he met his lawyer's eyes. "They ain't weeds," he muttered. "They don't grow there. That's just where they choose to come out of the ground."

"Well, Mr. Durkin, I don't know what to tell you except that the Aukowies are gone. You won."

Goldman got up to leave and Durkin stopped him to ask whether he contacted Jeanette Thompson yet about getting back his contract and the Book of Aukowies. Goldman told him he'd do it later that week, then nodded, his lopsided grin fixed in place as he left the room.

Durkin lay in bed troubled by the lawyer's visit. It didn't make sense that the Aukowies would've stopped coming out of Lorne Field days before the first frost. They'd never done that before, and he couldn't imagine why they were doing it now. If they could've been wiped out as easily as by setting the field on fire, it would've been done over three hundred years ago. Earlier, really, 'cause an Indian tribe had weeded the field for God knows how many years before the responsibility fell on the town, and then on the Durkin family. It just made no sense that they'd be gone. Everything in the contract was written for a reason, and he couldn't help feeling unsettled wondering what had happened to the Aukowies.

It was hours later when the state's psychiatrist came to talk to him. She was a small, owlish-looking woman in her early forties, but there was a gentleness and quietness to her that Durkin appreciated. Still, he didn't think it was fair for her to be evaluating him while he was doped up on morphine and worrying about the Aukowies, and he told her so. He mostly ignored her questions, not that she asked many. After waiting several minutes for him to respond to her last question, she smiled gently at him and told him he wasn't being fair himself and that she was told he was willing to cooperate with her. She spoke in a soft lisp, and the sound of it made him drowsy.

"I still don't think you should be talking to me until I'm off the morphine," he complained.

She smiled at that. "Jack, rest assured that your being on pain medication won't have any effect on my evaluation." She paused for a moment before continuing again in her soft lisp. "I am curious about something," she said. "It seems to me that you're the only person in your town who believes that these weeds are monsters. Is that true?"

"I never said they're monsters," Durkin muttered indignantly. "Monsters are unknown imaginary things. Aukowies have been well documented."

"Excuse me for my mistake. Are you the only person from your town who believes Aukowies grow out of Lorne Field?"

"Used to be the whole town believed that."

"But how about now?"

Durkin's jaw muscles hardened as he thought about it. "My son, Bert, believed it," he said finally. "He came down to the field the day he died to help me with my weeding. He could see their faces. He told me he could hear the cries they made when I killed them."

The psychiatrist nodded gently. She pulled her chair closer to Durkin's bed so she could hold his hand with both of hers. He didn't fight it, just turned his head away from her, his lips pressing into two thin bloodless lines.

"Do you think your son might've been telling you that to please you?"

"No, Bert believed it. I could tell. He wasn't humoring me."

"Maybe he made himself believe it as a way to please you?"

"It wasn't just Bert," Durkin said. "Hank Thompson told me he believed it, too. He told me how he snuck down to Lorne Field when he was a kid and watched my grandpa weeding the field. He heard the Aukowies scream when they died. He told me how he was afraid his ears were going to start bleeding from the noise."

The psychiatrist patted Durkin's hand. He kept his stare fixed on the opposite wall.

"Jack, as you said before, when Mr. Thompson was younger everyone in your town believed in these creatures. Naturally, Mr. Thompson would be predisposed to believe in them also. He knew he was supposed to hear them scream, so he heard them. This type of behavior is really the basis of group hysteria. Think of how a cult works. Everyone knows they're expected to believe, so they try hard to, and in the end they do believe, regardless of how irrational the beliefs are."

"I thought cults used brainwashing," Durkin muttered.

"That is all part of the psychology behind brainwashing," she said. "Think of what your town underwent for several hundred years as collective brainwashing."

Durkin shook his head slowly, his eyes still fixed on the opposite wall. "I know what I've been seeing my whole life," he said.

"Jack, think about it. The two most important male role models in your life were your father and grandfather. They both believed in these weeds being creatures, so you had to make yourself believe. You were going to see what you had to see and hear what you had to hear."

"It ain't like that," he said. "No, that ain't it. It don't explain why no animal, bird or insect goes anywhere near that field. It don't explain what I saw those Aukowies do to my son, Lester, or to Dan Wolcott."

"It does, Jack, if you think about it honestly. With everyone else in town doubting the existence of these creatures, you needed to believe, Jack. You needed to create those memories so you could continue to believe."

The muscles along Durkin's mouth and jaw bunched up as he shook his head. The psychiatrist waited patiently for him to speak. When he didn't she gently patted his hand again.

"What if Dan Wolcott's body still exists?" she asked.

"It don't. I saw what the Aukowies did to him."

"But what if it does? According to your statement, you waited forty minutes after Dan Wolcott stepped into the field before you set fire to his jeep. What if you used those forty minutes to drive his body somewhere?"

He shrugged. "If that happened, then I guess I'm crazy."

"Why don't I try to find out?"

Durkin looked back at her, his eyes staring unfocused into the distance. He nodded glumly.

❧

When the psychiatrist met later with McGrale and Goldman, she explained to them how she couldn't hypnotize Durkin.

"I thought I had him under," she told them. "But I guess I couldn't get him under deep enough." Sighing, she added, "Not everybody can be hypnotized."

"What makes you think you couldn't get him under deep enough?" McGrale asked.

"Because I couldn't tap into his unconscious. I was stuck in his false memories of watching the victim being torn apart by the weeds, and then with him spending the next forty minutes trying to figure out how to deal with the weeds. I couldn't budge him away from the field. I couldn't get him to remember what he did with the victim's body."

"Would additional hypnotherapy sessions work?" McGrale asked.

"Not in my professional opinion, no. He either can't be hypnotized and is faking, or the false memories are locked in too tightly."

McGrale rubbed his jaw. Goldman asked whether she'd support his client being declared incompetent.

"Absolutely not. He's lucid and, outside of his fantasies about those weeds, quite rational. I would oppose any attempt to do so."

"How about whether he's criminally insane?" McGrale asked, a pained look spreading over his face.

"He could be. He does believe these weeds are monsters. I have no doubt about that, and it's possible he murdered and disposed of the victim without any conscious awareness of it for no other reason than to erase self-doubts he may have been having about the true nature of those weeds. It's equally possible that this could be a calculated act to convince others of the existence of these monsters. This is a man who badly needs other people to believe this. The lack of respect he has been receiving in his Caretaker role has been devastating for him, especially since he feels as if he has been sacrificing his life for the world's sake. For that reason, and because I find it curious that his only supporters are both dead, I'm leaning more towards the latter explanation."

McGrale stood up, walked around his desk to where Goldman was sitting hunched over, and clapped the younger attorney solidly on the shoulder.

"Well, counsellor," he said. "For better or worse we'll be bringing this three-ring circus to the courtroom. Charges will be filed tomorrow."

That night Goldman visited Durkin to tell him about the arraignment hearing the next day and also that he went to see Jeanette Thompson, but that she claimed she never saw either the contract or book, and doubted whether they even existed. The news devastated Durkin. He sank back into his hospital bed an old man. Goldman was going to ask him for names of anyone else who might've ever seen either of those items, more to satisfy his own curiosity than anything else, but one look at Durkin and he knew it would be worse than beating an already whipped dog.

The next day Durkin was taken to the District Court in an ambulance and wheeled into the courthouse with a blanket covering the lower part of his body. The reporters and photographers lined up outside pressed towards him, but he stared blindly ahead and gave them no notice. Inside the courtroom he was charged with manslaughter in the first degree and remanded without bail. When the trial date was set for April tenth, Durkin grabbed Goldman by his over-sized suit jacket and pulled him close.

"That's too late," he croaked frantically. "That's going to be at least two weeks after spring thaw. If the Aukowies are left alone for that long—"

"Please, Mr. Durkin, let go of my suit," Goldman whispered, grimacing. "And don't worry about the Aukowies. If they're what you say they are it will only help our case."

"Help our case? You don't understand a thing. If they get too big there ain't nothin' anyone can do about them."

"I'll be checking on them everyday, Mr. Durkin, don't worry. Please, let go of my suit."

Durkin noticed people in the courtroom staring at him. He let go of Goldman's suit jacket, his face flushing a deep red. As he was wheeled out, he caught sight of Lydia sitting in the courtroom watching him. Lester, also. In the back row was Jeanette Thompson looking at him as if he were a bug. He pretended not to see any of them.

A week later Durkin was fitted with a prosthetic foot and, after another two weeks of physical therapy, was brought back to a cell in the County Jail. It was December second when Goldman visited him, telling him he had some good news. Lester had recanted his earlier testimony and was now saying that the Aukowies bit off his thumb.

"So they believe me?" Durkin said, excitement rising cautiously in his eyes. "They goin' to let me out of here and give me my old Caretaker job back?"

"Well, no. People are looking at this as a son trying to help his father. It won't have any impact on the manslaughter charges against you for Sheriff Wolcott, but it will force them to drop the aggravated assault charges against you for your son's injury. As much as they'd like to, they can't proceed with a trial without your son's testimony."

Durkin sat back on his jail cot, his face deflating. "That's all you got for me?"

"Well, no." Goldman's lopsided grin grew large as he took a manila folder out of his briefcase. "I found a copy of your Caretaker's contract and the Book of Aukowies. Thought you'd like to see it."

Durkin's eyes filled with tears as he flipped through each

page. When he looked up at Goldman, his leathery face was
on the verge of crumbling.

"How'd you get this?" he asked.

"I talked with your wife earlier today. She told me that
a lawyer she saw a while back made this copy, so I saw him
and he gave it to me. Hope you don't mind, but I made a
copy for myself. Fascinating reading, by the way. I'm planning to use it for our case."

Durkin shook his head while rubbing a hand across his
eyes. He wiped his hand off on his shirt and held it out to his
attorney, who only hesitated for a moment before taking it.

"I don't know why this means so much to me anymore,
but it does," Jack Durkin said. "Thanks."

Goldman nodded solemnly and left the Caretaker alone
with his contract and book.

Lydia visited the next day. Both of them stared stonily at
each other until Lydia broke the ice, telling Durkin that she
couldn't stomach the idea of seeing him until Lester told the
truth about him not cutting off his son's thumb.

"Don't think for a second I believe any of that Aukowie
nonsense," she said. "But I accept that it happened because
of an accident."

"How are you, Lydia?"

"I-I'm good," she stammered, surprised at the question.
"I got a nice apartment. Lester's with me now. If you can
believe it, some idiot publisher from New York is paying me
a ton of money to write a book. Guess what it's going to be
called?"

"I don't know."

"The Caretaker's Wife." She took a heavy breath and

added, "This business with Daniel is getting me invitations on all these shows to promote it. I'm on Oprah next week, and Letterman the week after, if you can believe it."

"Hard to picture."

"Ain't it?" She sniffed, dry-eyed, and tried to smile, but it broke. "Jack, why don't you tell them what you did to Daniel's body? Your lawyer told me if you do you'll only have to serve ten years."

"I wish I could," Durkin said, showing only a bare trace of a smile. "The problem is I'm telling it the way I remember it. What do you think of my lawyer?"

"He seems smart."

"You think so? To me, he's just a kid who can't even look me in the eye. I think he's afraid of me." Durkin laughed at that. "I only got one foot and he's afraid of me. Thinks I'm crazy. He's having me see a psychiatrist now who's trying to convince me I'm crazy, too. According to him I killed Dan and hid his body without knowing it, that I did it so I could *continue living in my fantasy-world concerning the Aukowies*. Maybe he's right."

"All those years alone in that field were bound to drive you crazy," she said. "Ain't entirely your fault. I guess I could've been better to you."

"No, you couldn't've. I'm sorry I married you, Lydia."

She stared hotly at him, her jaw dropping open. "Why, you old fool! Here I am trying to be nice to you—"

"I didn't mean it that way. I mean because I married you only because of the contract. I needed to marry someone. But I didn't love you. And I know you didn't love me. I stole that from you. Because of me you never had a chance to marry someone out of love, and I'm sorry. But I did grow to care about you, even though we could barely tolerate each other."

Tears leaked from Lydia's eyes. She turned away trying to hide it. "No doubt about it," she said. "You have gone completely crazy."

"God, I hope so. I'm praying every day that I'm insane. It's the only chance the world has."

"Don't worry, you're crazy," she said. She paused to wipe a thin hand across her eyes. "Is it okay if Lester visits you? He'd really like to."

"I'd like that, too. And Lydia, I'm so sorry about Bert."

She bit her lip and nodded, fighting back her tears.

"Lester's waiting in the car," she said. "I'll send him in here to see you. You take care, you old fool."

Hiding her face from him, she rushed out of the visitor's area.

Lester wore a despondent look as he entered the room, his hands shoved deep in his pockets. He nodded towards his father, kicking at the floor as he walked over to his chair.

"I'm sorry, dad," he said.

"I know, son."

"I'm sorry for throwing those tomatoes at you."

"Were you the one who hit me square in the nose?"

Lester nodded solemnly.

"You have a good arm. You almost knocked me to the ground."

"I'm sorry, dad."

"No more sorries, okay?"

Lester shook his head. "I still got to say how sorry I am for telling people you cut off my thumb."

"It's over, Lester."

"I'm still so sorry. You lost our house because of that.

And everything else that happened . . . to you . . . to Bert . . . It was all my fault. I just couldn't remember anything about what happened to me, and when they asked me to say those things I went along because I didn't want to be Caretaker. I'm so sorry, dad."

"So you don't remember Aukowies biting off your thumb?"

Lester shook his head.

"You just said that to help me out?"

"Yeah."

"Son, come closer."

Lester wiped a hand under his nose and hesitantly stepped forward. Jack Durkin grabbed him and hugged his son close to his chest. He let go only when he realized Lester was struggling to maintain his composure and would be bawling soon.

"Okay, son," he said, "you better go back out with your ma. Take good care of her, okay?"

Lester nodded morosely, his mouth forming a tiny circle on his pale face. Durkin watched him leave and wondered why he was so disappointed. If Lester had truly seen the Aukowies bite off his thumb, then the world was damned. As it was, there was still a glimmer of hope his psychiatrist's angle on it was right—that the Aukowies existed only in his mind. At least he could hope for the best.

Chapter 14

Spring thaw occurred on March twentieth the next year. Every day after, Goldman came to see Jack Durkin to tell him nothing was growing on Lorne Field. That the place was still as desolate as the moon. He seemed disappointed, almost as if he was hoping to see monsters there, or maybe for some reason he didn't want to accept a solution as mundane as Durkin just being insane.

During the months leading up to his trial, Durkin hoped that Wolcott's body would be found. If that happened, then he could accept that he was in fact insane and at least be assured that the world would be safe. But as much as he wanted to, he couldn't shake a growing uneasiness that his memories were real. That he was not brainwashed. That he was not the victim of collective hysteria. That he didn't have the psychotic breakdowns that his psychiatrist insisted he did. That the Aukowies were real, and that his violations of the contract had irrevocably altered the equation with them. He couldn't shake his uneasiness that burning them alive was the final straw and that they were no longer playing by the rules that the contract governed.

Everything in that contract is written for a reason, his pa used to tell him. *You have to cherish it, treat is as the most sacred document on the planet . . .*

Instead he had violated it. Over and over again. If the Aukowies were real, how could burning one generation stop all those other generations from pushing their way up? If they were real, then somehow he had damned the world . . . If they were just weeds, then none of it mattered.

He prayed that they were just weeds. As much as he didn't want to be insane, he prayed that he was. He wondered whether someone insane would feel as he did.

During those winter months, Durkin read every book he could get his hands on. His lawyer helped him by bringing in stacks of books every time he visited. Homer, Steinbeck, Twain, Plato, Dickens, Shakespeare, Milton, Cervantes—he found himself particularly drawn to *Don Quixote*. But it was Dante's *Divine Comedy* that made him tremble as he read it. As a kid he never bothered to read books, since he knew from the start what was planned for him, and later, after he became Caretaker, he was either too tired during the months between spring thaw and first frost, or simply needed to rest during the winter months to regain his strength. Now, though, he read insatiably and continuously as if he were trying to squeeze in a lifetime of reading. Even though Lydia's book made the New York Times bestseller's list, his lawyer never brought it, and he never asked for it.

Eventually his trial came. His lawyer had blown up drawings from the Book of Aukowies to postersize and introduced them as evidence to show the jury how Durkin had been indoctrinated in support of his temporary insanity defense.

On the first day of the trial, he whispered to Durkin how they were going on day twenty since spring thaw. "I've been out there every day, and nothing's growing," he said, his grin strained. There was an edginess to him, a discomfort. Durkin knew that the lawyer had read both the contract and the Book of Aukowies carefully, and as much as he wanted to believe that it was a simple matter of Durkin having a psychotic breakdown, he had his own doubts. He mentioned to Durkin several times over the winter how he couldn't fathom Durkin cutting off Wolcott's foot with a single slice of the machete. He told Durkin how he had bought the same brand of machete and tried himself with a watermelon and couldn't cut it through with one strike. "We're talking a watermelon, Mr. Durkin. Somehow you were supposed to cut through a leather boot and bone. I don't see how you did it." When Durkin found himself thinking about it, he couldn't see how he could've done it, either. But he tried not to think about it. He tried to think that it was a simple matter of that psychiatrist being right. Or maybe somehow burning a field of Aukowies alive ended them forever. Maybe that was it. Except everything in the contract was written for a reason. His pa said so. So did his grandpa. And his great grandpa before him . . .

Durkin had trouble paying attention to his trial. He was too distracted to understand what people were saying. He was too uneasy. He could tell his lawyer was feeling the same way, but it didn't stop Goldman from whispering to him that they were going on day twenty-three . . .

It was on the fourth day of his trial when he heard the screams, along with everybody else in the courtroom. They were short-lived and followed by a weird kind of popping noise—kind of like an amplified bug zapper. People in the courtroom rushed to the windows, then started screaming themselves. Durkin sat where he was. His lawyer just stared at him, his grin folding into a frightened grimace.

It didn't take long for the Aukowies to bust through the walls. Seconds maybe. They were exactly as in the drawings. Nine feet long with evil horned faces and fangs everywhere.

One of them hovered in front of Durkin, its open jaws unhinging inches from his face. It recognized him, and he knew he would be saved for last. Instead it buzzed through Goldman, turning his lawyer into nothing but pink spray. Durkin felt bad seeing it. Over the last several months he had grown to like him. As much as he wanted to kid himself otherwise, he had known all along what had happened. When he burned the Aukowies alive he changed everything. Instead of coming up in Lorne Field, they chose someplace else. Someplace quiet. Maybe it took longer, twenty-three days to be exact, but at least they wouldn't be burnt alive where they pushed through the ground.

Unless he truly was insane.

He closed his eyes and wished that that was the case. That the screams and popping noises he heard were the sounds that an insane man would hear. That the moist spray hitting his face was just the sensation that someone out of his mind would imagine. He prayed that that was what it was. After he was done praying, he begged for forgiveness.

I'm so sorry, he thought. *Lydia, Lester, I'm sorry for what's going to happen to you. But it wasn't fair. It just isn't right to put this kind of burden on one man's shoulders. You had no right doing it.*

With a smile, he realized how crazy that was. A man bitterly complaining to a God he didn't believe in. It gave him some hope. But under no circumstance was he going to open his eyes.